MEXICAN TREASURE

Randita looked at the shallow river and said, "I think I will bathe, Longarm. I am dirty from where I have been kept, much dirtier than the clean desert dust that has blown on us today."

"Go ahead," Longarm told her. "I'll just stretch out here and shut my eyes while you're bathing, so as you won't feel embarrassed."

Though he'd only intended to rest, he dropped off to sleep. A soft hand on his face aroused him, and when he looked up he saw Randita had knelt by his side. She had not put on her clothes after bathing, and when she bent forward to kiss him, her full breasts pressed on his chest.

"If you figure you owe me something for giving you a hand back at Calderon's place, you're wrong," he said.

"I was not thinking of debts or payments," she replied. "I was thinking of you as a man . . ."

— TABOR EVANS —

LONGARM
AND THE
MEXICAN LINE-UP

A JOVE BOOK

LONGARM AND THE MEXICAN LINE-UP

A Jove Book/published by arrangement with
the author

PRINTING HISTORY
Jove edition/January 1987

ISBN: 0-515-08838-2

Jove Books are published by the Berkley Publishing Group,
200 Madison Avenue, New York, N.Y. 10016. The words
"A JOVE BOOK" and the "J" with sunburst are trademarks
belonging to Jove Publications, Inc.

PRINTED IN THE UNITED STATES OF AMERICA

Chapter 1

A shot cracked from the sagebrush that grew in scattered clumps on all sides of the draw and the slug chipped at the edge of the shallow hollow between Longarm and his prisoner. The bullet whizzed through the little spurt of dust it had raised and thunked into the opposite wall of the earth-crease in which the two had finally found shelter.

Longarm did not fire in response to the shot, but both he and the prisoner hugged the ground a little closer. The single shot was followed by a small volley as all three of the outlaws who'd run them to cover joined in the shooting. Longarm glanced over his shoulder to make sure neither of the horses had been hit, then returned his attention to the handcuffed man who was stretched out beside him against the slanting side of the draw.

"Well, Yeager," he said drily, "It looks to me like your friends out there's got all the ammunition they need, or they wouldn't be wasting it that way."

"You know as well as I do that a hardcase on the prod's got to carry plenty of shells," No-Nose Yeager grunted. "When a man gets on the dodge, he can't just walk into any store he comes to and buy him a box of bullets."

At some early point during Yeager's career he'd gotten into a knife fight from which he'd emerged second best. During the duel, his opponent's blade had sliced into his nose at the beginning of the soft cartilage below its bridge and traveled down to his upper lip, removing his nostrils.

1

The skin had grown back to cover the area of severed flesh, but the triangle of scar tissue that ran from just below his eyes to his upper lip did not tan to match his bronzed cheeks and jaws.

With the scar added to his thin eyebrows, fathomless black eyes, high cheekbones, and thin lips, Yeager's face, shaded by his battered, low-crowned hat, looked for all the world like a skull. Every time he looked at the man beside him, Longarm got the impression that he was staring at the face of death.

Now the outlaw held out his wrists, joined by the chain of Longarm's handcuffs, and suggested, "If you'd take these damn things off and lend me that Colt of yours, I'd sure be tickled to help you stand 'em off."

"I ain't all that big of a fool, Yeager," Longarm replied firmly. "If push comes to shove, I ain't real certain you'd be on my side all the way. For all I know, you got the word that your friends were going to try to help you before we left Greybull this morning."

Yeager's trial had ended the day before in a special federal court that had convened for the occasion in Greybull, near the northern border of Wyoming Territory. From the beginning there had been no doubt what the verdict would be, but because of Greybull's size and isolation, the judge had not ordered Yeager to be hanged immediately following the end of the trial.

Instead, he had set the execution date two weeks in the future and ordered that it take place in the Territorial capital at Casper, where a regular gallows was already installed in the prison. Since Longarm had been the arresting officer, the judge had given him the duty of transporting Yeager to Casper.

Starting from Greybull at dawn on horses rented from the local livery stable, the two had covered perhaps a dozen miles before sighting the three riders who were streaking toward them in pursuit. Yeager had recognized

2

them from a distance, but until Longarm prodded him with the muzzle of his Colt, Yeager had refused to identify them. At last he had admitted reluctantly that only members of the gang to which he had belonged would have any reason to follow them.

"They're coming to get me away from you, Long," Yeager had boasted. "You'd best just let me go now and cut a shuck while you still got a chance to get away from them."

"Running ain't my style," Longarm had answered tersely. "I don't give up a prisoner all that easy."

"They ain't gonna ride up to you and ask you to let me go, you know," the condemned outlaw had grinned. The skewed smile on his face twisted his lips and made his face look more like a skull than ever. "They'll whipsaw you between 'em, and come at you from three ways, all at the same time. Why, you won't have the chance of a snowball in hell!"

Yeager's hopes had been blasted when the trio in pursuit of them had started firing even before they got within range.

"Damn it!" he'd frowned. "As far as they are, they can't tell which one of us is which! They're out to get me and you both!"

"I ain't surprised," Longarm had replied. "Likely they got the idea that a man who's talked once ain't going to find it hard to talk a lot more. They'd rather see you dead with your mouth shut than alive and talking about the jobs you pulled with 'em."

"Well, why ain't you shooting back?" Yeager had demanded. "I'm your prisoner! You got to protect me!"

"Don't worry. I ain't carrying but a handful of shells for my Winchester, and I can't waste 'em. But we'll hole up and I'll fight 'em off, the first cover we come to."

As the riders pursuing them continued to gain ground, and the bullets they let off began to kick up dust uncomfortably close, Longarm had halted in the only cover they had encountered, the little gully in which they were now holed up.

"This place ain't such a much, but it'll keep us from being sitting ducks for them friends of yours," Longarm had told his prisoner. "Now, you just keep in mind who started shooting at you, and don't try no stunts on me."

"Maybe I ain't altogether on your side, Long," Yeager grunted, his voice as sour as his breath. "But from what I told about 'em, all the jobs they pulled while I was riding alongside of 'em, you sure oughta know by now that I ain't on their side, either."

"So you say," Longarm told him skeptically. "I been a U. S. marshal long enough by now to know how your kind hangs together."

"There ain't no such thing as hanging together when a man from what you call my kind stands up in court and gives sworn testimony agin his pals," Yeager said slowly. "Once he's done that, there ain't nobody he can hang on to. Not even the law, if it comes down to it."

"I don't see as how you—" Longarm broke off as another quick volley of shots sounded from the rolling, brushy land that stretched away in all directions from the gully.

This time the outlaws seemed more determined than ever to bring their attack to a close, for they continued shooting sporadically for several minutes. The rifles barked so fast and so continuously during the few moments their barrage lasted that Longarm was unable to count the separate reports. From the long silence which followed before the renegades who had them cornered resumed shooting, Longarm was sure that all three of them had emptied the magazines of their weapons.

When they began firing once more, Longarm waited until the guns had again fallen silent. Then he levered himself quickly above the rim of the little gully, his rifle ready. In the few seconds required for him to shoulder the Win-

4

chester, his eyes had flicked across the terrain occupied by the outlaws. As he'd figured, all three of them were busy reloading.

Picking his target while the renegades were still sliding shells into the magazines of their rifles, Longarm let off a shot. The outlaw he'd put in his sights jerked back in his saddle when the deadly slug found its target. His rifle slid from his lifeless hands as he crumpled forward. Then he toppled from his saddle like a big tree felled by a woodsman's axe and lay motionless on the sunbaked earth.

Before the two remaining attackers could bring up their weapons, Longarm had dropped flat against the wall of the gully. He'd barely gotten down before slugs again thunked into the desert soil. A few cleared the edge of the depression, whistling above the heads of Longarm and Yeager, and spatted angrily into the bank behind them. The result was the same that had come from the earlier shots; none of the outlaws' bullets found a mark.

"Sounded to me like you taken one of 'em down," Yeager observed as the echoes of the volley died away. He hadn't lifted his head to look when Longarm popped up to shoot. "There was only two rifles spit."

Longarm nodded, then said, "Your old friends out there ain't very smart. If they'd split up and come at us from both sides at the same time, we'd be goners."

"Don't be so damn anxious," Yeager retorted. "They'll think about doing just that after a while."

Longarm raised his head above the edge of the gully once again to check on the movements of the remaining two outlaws. No shot greeted his move and he quickly saw why. They had pulled their horses close together and one of them was gesturing with a hand, the second man listening and nodding.

"From the way they're palavering, I'd say they got the idea of splitting up," he told Yeager without taking his eyes off the pair of outlaws.

"Mind if I lift up and take a look?"

5

"What good is that going to do you?"

"Not a bit, I reckon," Yeager replied. "I'm curious to know, is all."

"Go ahead and look, then," Longarm agreed. "Just don't let your curiosity get the best of you, though. It's my job to get you to the pen alive, and I aim to do just that."

Yeager braced himself and pushed his head up quickly to peer over the gully's rim. He dropped back an instant before a shot cracked and a rifle slug whined through the air where his head had appeared. Yeager shook his head sorrowfully.

"I didn't ever think I'd live to see it," he said.

"See what?"

"Well, one of them fellows is Pete Dover. Now, it didn't surprise me none to see Pete out there. He's new to the bunch, and me and him never did get what you'd call well acquainted. But the other one's Stud Barrow, and Stud and me was buddies for a long time. We stood side by side on maybe fifteen or more jobs before you busted up our bunch."

"And that was him, the one that just taken a shot when he seen you?"

"Yep." Yeager was silent for a moment, then went on, "I don't know as I could stand to take a shot at Stud, after all the things we was in together."

"It don't look like he feels the same way about you that you do about him," Longarm suggested. "He's sure trying to close your book."

"It don't make me feel good to admit it, but I guess you're the only one that can keep him from doing just that," Yeager agreed. He hunkered down a bit lower in the gully and added, "I ain't asking to help you, Long, but it don't make me feel good to see old Stud out there trying to cut my water off. If you want me to do anything to help you, I'll oblige you."

"I don't figure to need no help from the likes of you, Yeager," Longarm replied, his voice cold. "There's only the two of your old friends out there now, and I'll do my own fighting. All I want you to do is set still right where you are and keep outa my way."

Another barrage of shots broke the prairie's stillness before Yeager could reply. In the silence that followed, Longarm risked lifting his head for another look. As he'd suspected would be the case, one of the outlaws was walking his horse back to place him in line with the center of the gully where Longarm and Yeager were holed up. The other had whipped his horse to a gallop and was preparing to circle in a wide arc around the little cleft, which would place the two renegades in position to catch the gully in a crossfire.

Longarm made a quick estimate of the amount of time the rider would need to get in place. To avoid taking a rifle bullet at close range, the outlaw had ridden well beyond the point where the slit in the ground narrowed to nothing. Longarm guessed that he had three or four minutes to act. He turned to Yeager.

"Pull one of your boots off," he commanded.

Yeager stared slack-jawed for a moment, a frown forming on his face. "One of my boots?" he asked. "What in—"

"Damn it, stop jawing and do what I said!"

His face showing his bewilderment, the outlaw levered off one of his boots and held it out.

"I don't want the damn thing!" Longarm snapped. "Pick up that stick on the ground in front of you and put it in your boot, then turn it upside down and fix your hat on the sole."

Comprehension now showed on Yeager's face. "I catch on now," he nodded as he obeyed Longarm's commands. "Where you want me to be when I lift it up above the rim of the gully?"

"Right where you are is good enough."

Longarm spoke over his shoulder as he took a couple of short steps away from Yeager. The move gave him the

7

scanty shelter of a bush that grew on the rim of the gully at his back.

"Now, I ain't so sure this old trick's going to fool them friends of yours. They've likely used it theirselves, but when a man ain't got no more choice than we have, he'll try damn near anything."

"Just tell me when you're ready," Yeager said tersely.

"No use that I can see in waiting," Longarm told him. He shifted his grip on the rifle to hold it in a position which would allow him to bring it to his shoulder instantly, then looked again at Yeager and went on, "That fellow circling us is going to be in place in about another minute or two. Go ahead and poke it up."

Yeager lifted the hat-topped boot slowly, in the manner a cautious man might move when he lifted his head to peer over the gully's rim.

Longarm watched him for a second or so, thinking that even at such close range the boot on which the hat rested gave the effect of being a man's face shaded by the broad hatbrim. Then he shifted his attention to the area in front of him. He saw the mounted outlaw's head turn as the motion of the rising hat caught his eyes.

Shouldering his Winchester as he stood up and inched forward for a clear shot, Longarm got the mounted desperado in his sights and triggered off his shot. The outlaw saw him, but by then the deadly lead from the rifle was already whizzing toward him.

True to Longarm's aim, the bullet took him in the left side of his chest and tore through his heart. The outlaw's rifle cracked, but its muzzle was already sagging downward and the slug did nothing more than kick up dust a few yards from his horse's hooves. Then the outlaw toppled out of his saddle and lay still on the sunbaked earth.

As though it was an echo, another rifle barked. Longarm swiveled with catlike speed, but the mounted outlaw got off a second shot before Longarm could aim and fire. Then Longarm got the man in his rifle sights, and his

8

aim was as true as it had been before. The slug from his rifle was as effective as the first, even though this time he was firing at a moving target. The rider's body jerked and his arms flew wide, his rifle falling to the ground. He slumped in his saddle and then slid slowly to one side and hit the ground a few feet from the weapon. He rolled once from the momentum of his fall. After that he lay motionless.

Only after the echoes of the gunfire died away did Longarm realize that Yeager had been hit. When he looked away from the body of the rider, he saw that his prisoner had dropped the decoying hat and was pawing at his chest with his manacled hands. Before Longarm could reach him, Yeager lurched forward and collapsed, falling facedown against the slanted wall of the crevice. Two long steps brought Longarm to the outlaw's side.

"How bad're you hit?" he asked.

"I ain't sure," Yeager gasped. "All I know is I'm burning like hell inside my chest."

Glancing at his prisoner's back, Longarm could see the reason. Below the bulge of flesh formed by the exit of the rifle slug, blood was spreading in a widening stain on Yeager's shirt.

"Just stand still and don't try to move," Longarm told him.

Two long strides took him to Yeager's horse. He pulled his pocketknife from his pocket as he moved. It was open in his hand when he reached the animal. Lifting a corner of its saddle blanket, Longarm slashed at the tough canvas of the saddle pad until he had cut a broad triangle off one of its corners. Then he cut off the horse's dangling reins and returned to Yeager's side. The outlaw was still lying motionless, his chest heaving as he gasped for breath.

"Bandages is one thing I don't carry," Longarm said. "But maybe I can lash up something that'll keep you from bleeding so bad. Lift up as much as you can while I see what I can do."

9

Yeager braced himself in a half-erect posture, leaning on the side of the gully. Longarm slashed away the outlaw's shirt and looked at the little purple-rimmed hole where the rifle slug had torn into his chest, then at the ugly gaping wound in his back where the bullet had torn away a big patch of skin and a chunk of flesh from which blood was draining profusely.

Pressing the saddle pad over the wound in Yeager's back, he wrapped the reins around the wounded man's chest to hold it in place, and pulled the leathers as tight as he could before knotting them to squeeze the pad over the wound. Yeager was trembling involuntarily by the time the crude bandage was in place. As Longarm stepped away from him, the outlaw sagged back against the slanting side of the gully.

"I'm making you no promises," he said. "But that oughta help stop you from bleeding so much. We'll rest for a little while and give the blood time to clot up and close that hole in your back."

"How bad off am I?" Yeager asked.

"Well, I seen men live that's been wounded as bad as you are, and I seen 'em die from a shot that didn't make more'n a little bitty hole going in and out. Damn it, Yeager, I ain't no doctor. You know how you feel better'n I do."

"Right now, I don't feel like I'm gonna make it," the outlaw said, his voice shaky. "But maybe it's like you said, give that blood time to clot up and quit draining out, and I'll feel a little bit better."

Longarm nodded. Though he knew Yeager exactly for the outlaw and murderer he was, Longarm was like all lawmen—he hated to lose a prisoner who'd been put in his custody.

"Just stay still," he told Yeager. "I got almost a full bottle of whiskey in my saddlebag. I'll get it and maybe you'll perk up a mite after you've had a shot."

Walking to his horse, Longarm opened his saddlebag

10

and took out the bottle of Tom Moore that he'd bought the evening before. He was turning away when Yeager called to him.

"Long! While you're there at your saddlebag, will you do something for me?"

"Like what?"

"When the jailer in Greybull handed me over to you, I seen him give you that sack of stuff I had in my pockets when they brought me in. Would you bring it back with you? There's—" A bout of coughing seized the wounded man and left him gasping.

"All right," Longarm told him. "I guess it won't hurt nothing to let you have your own personal belongings."

Rummaging in his saddlebag again, Longarm pulled out the little cloth sack which contained whatever had been in Yeager's pockets at the time of his arrest. Carrying the sack in one hand and the whiskey in the other, he returned to Yeager.

"Put away a good swallow of this," he said, handing the whiskey bottle to the wounded man. "Maybe it'll perk you up."

Yeager took the bottle. The handcuffs forced him to hold it in both hands while he tilted it up and drank. He swallowed clumsily, a trickle of the sharp-edged Maryland rye escaping his lips as he pulled the bottle away. A gurgling cough shook him, and he handed the bottle back to Longarm.

Longarm wiped the bottle neck and tilted it to his lips. He felt that he deserved a drink, too, after the gunfight. He kept his eyes on Yeager while he swallowed, and could see the outlaw was beginning to revive a bit as the potent liquor took its effect. Corking the bottle and placing it on the ground, he handed Yeager the sack containing his personal effects.

After fumbling for a moment with the drawstrings, Yeager managed to open the sack. He slid one hand into it and took out a gold hunting-cased watch. He stared at it for a moment, then lifted his head to look at Longarm.

"This here's about all I got that's worth anything," he said. His voice was a bit stronger now, the whiskey doing its work. "And I ain't got no youngsters that I know about to pass it on to. Matter, of fact, all the kith and kin I got is a niece, but she's a sweet little girl, and I set a lot of store in her."

When Yeager paused and gasped for breath, Longarm handed him the bottle again. The outlaw drank and coughed, and when he wiped his mouth with the back of his hand Longarm saw that the phlegm he'd brought up was streaked with threads of blood.

"You don't owe me nothing, Long," Yeager went on. "But I figure I'm a goner. You're the kind of man that'll keep his word if he gives it to a fellow that's dying."

Another bout of coughing shook the outlaw's body. Longarm could do nothing except watch.

When he could speak again, Yeager continued, "I'm going to ask you one thing, Long. When I die, take this watch and give it to my niece. Tell her it's all I had to pass on to her. Now, will you do that much of a favor for me?"

Longarm looked at the watch in Yeager's outstretched hand. He asked, "How come you're trying to saddle me with a job like that, Yeager? Except that I'm the only one around?"

"I've heard enough about you to figure you'll keep your word, even if it's just an outlaw like me that you've give it to," Yeager replied. "How about it, Long? Will you do it?"

Chapter 2

Before Longarm could answer, Yeager was seized by another bout of coughing. More blood spattered from his mouth as his body shook. He hawked and spat, his chest heaving as he gasped for breath. Longarm could see that there was very little time left to the wounded man. Reluctantly, he nodded.

"I reckon I owe you that much, Yeager," he said slowly. "Seeing as how it's sorta my fault that you was shot. Tell me about this niece of yours. What's her name, and how do you expect me to find her?"

"Her name's Taffeta Pearson," Yeager said after he'd taken three or four gasping breaths. "But folks just calls her Taffy. The last time I seen her was just before you snagged me for that bank job me and the gang pulled. That'd've been about four months ago, and she was in Rock Springs, working in a saloon called the Owlhoot."

"Four months in one place for a girl in that line of work is a long time," Longarm frowned. "You sure she's still there?"

"I figure she is," the outlaw nodded. His voice was raspy now, and little more than a hoarse whisper. "If she ain't, she oughta be someplace close by. Anyhow, a man in your job's used to tracking folks dow, Long. I don't guess you'll have much trouble finding her."

Overcoming his reluctance, Longarm nodded slowly and said, "All right. It ain't going to be much outa my way

13

to swing by Rock Springs on the way back to Denver. I'll see that she gets the watch, and whatever's left in this bag of stuff that's yours."

"It ain't much," Yeager said, trying to smile. His voice was thready now, and his breathing even more raspingly strained. "But the watch is the main thing I want Taffy to have. It belonged to my daddy, Taffy's grandpa. I don't reckon it's worth a whole lot, but I'd as leif keep it in the family."

"You got my word," Longarm nodded. He held out the bottle of Tom Moore. "But maybe you'll make it to hand it to her yourself. Take another swallow now, and lean back and shut your eyes and get some rest."

Yeager managed a twisted grin as he struggled to raise his hand to take the bottle. He gasped, "The only place I'm going to make it to is a six-by-three hole, Long. You know that just the same as I—"

Blood gushing from his lips cut the outlaw's words off in mid-sentence. His jaw went slack, his extended arm dropped and hung limp. His head fell forward and his body began sliding down the gully's steep wall until his crumpled form lay huddled on the baked ground of the little cleft's floor.

Longarm stood for a moment, looking at Yeager's lifeless body. Then he lifted the bottle to his lips and took two good-sized swallows. Corking the bottle, he fished one of his long, thin cigars from his vest pocket and flicked his thumbnail over the head to light a match.

Well, old son, he told himself silently as he looked at the three scattered bodies and the horses that stood patiently beside them, *looks like that judge up in Greybull handed you more of a job than either you or him figured it'd be. By the time you load these bodies on the horses and start moving, you'll be lucky to make it to Lander before it's too dark to see, so you better get cracking."*

• • •

Placing his saddlebags in an aisle seat of the smoking car and leaning his Winchester in the space between the window seat and the wall of the coach, Longarm lowered himself into the window seat just as the train began moving. During his overnight stay in the little railhead town of Lander, he'd had time to soak off the desert dust in a real bathtub and enjoy a respectable breakfast.

He looked out the window of the Chicago & Northern coach as the engine struggled to pick up speed before starting up the long slope of the Continental Divide. For the first time since leaving Greybull, Longarm allowed himself to relax. Until he reached Denver after the stop he would have to make in Rock Springs, he had only one minor responsibility—to deliver Yeager's watch to the dead outlaw's niece.

And that ought not to be such a much of a job, old son, he told himself, touching a match to a fresh cigar and leaning his head back against the seat's headrest. *Always providing you can find her. But you gave your word to Yeager, and you got to make a try. Funny a man like him would set so much store on a such a piddly little chore, but I guess when a fellow looks the devil in the eye it sorta changes how he thinks.*

Dipping his hand into the capacious pocket of his coat, Longarm took out the bag that contained Yeager's meager possessions and fished the watch from it. He turned it over and around, looking at the design of intertwined vines and leaves that covered its gold case, then held it to his ear. It was not ticking. Opening the case, he wound it carefully, and watched while the minute hand began its measured advance around the porcelain dial from the point at which it had stopped to the nearest Roman numeral.

This is a pretty good watch, at that, old son, he told himself, closing the case and holding the watch to the window to get a better look at the engraving.

A series of scratches at one point just below the stem

15

caught Longarm's eye. He brought it closer to his eyes and examined the scratched area more carefully.

Now, them scraped places looks right fresh, he mused. *If I ain't imagining something, Yeager pried the back open not too long ago. Question is, why'd he do it?*

Taking out his pocketknife, Longarm inserted the blade into the groove and twisted. The back snapped open, exposing the engine-turned steel plate that protected the mechanism. The quivering balance spring was not what caught his attention, however. Folded into the curved back of the case there was a scrap of tissue-thin paper.

Again Longarm brought his knife blade into play. He slid the point under the edge of the paper and lifted it from the case. When he laid the watch on the seat beside him and opened out the folds, he was holding a quarter-sheet of paper, so thin that it was translucent. On it were a few thin, carefully drawn lines with sets of numbers and letters at irregular intervals beside them.

"Damned if this ain't a map!" Longarm exclaimed under his breath. "And if I know outlaw ways, it's got to show places where that gang Yeager rode with has hid away their loot!"

Longarm studied the lines and the cryptic notations beside them for several minutes, but it seemed that the longer he tried to determine their meanings, the further he was from solving the puzzle they presented.

At last he gave up. He picked up the watch and was about to replace the paper where he had found it, but as he re-folded the paper a thought struck him. Closing the watch case, he put the timepiece in his coat pocket and took out the thin bifold wallet in which he carried his shield. Flipping it open, he slid the bit of paper into the compartment behind the shield. Then he leaned back in the green plush seat, closed his eyes, and dozed until the conductor called the Rock Springs station stop.

Peering out the window in the gathering dusk, he saw that the town had already begun to lose its one-street character. The last time he had seen Rock Springs was from the window of an eastbound Union Pacific daycoach. At that time the town had stretched in a single row of shanty-like houses parallel to the Union Pacific's rails. Now houses were strung out on both side of the UP tracks and were creeping along the new C&N right-of-way.

Daylight was almost gone when he swung off the train, and the lights from the windows of stores and saloons along the main street were glowing pale in the fading light. He glanced at the saloon signs until he found the one he was looking for. He did not go in, but turned back and headed for the Stockman's Hotel.

In his sparsely furnished second-floor room, Longarm shed his coat, took his bottle of Tom Moore out of his saddlebag, and downed a satisfying swig. Then, with a fresh cheroot clamped between his teeth, he started down the main street to begin his search for Yeager's niece.

In the first two saloons he tried, he drew blanks, but in the third he hit paydirt. This was a more imposing establishment than the first two. In addition to a chuck-a-luck layout and a poker table, it boasted a postage-stamp-sized dance floor and small tables for its patrons in the rear area, where scantily clad waitresses stood against the wall awaiting patrons.

At that early hour of the evening, the saloon was sparsely patronized. A trio of customers stood at the bar. The dealers had not yet taken their positions at the gaming tables, the dance floor was empty, and the tables for drinkers boasted only two or three patrons. Longarm chose an isolated corner table, ordered Tom Moore from the red-skirted waitress who bustled up, and waited until the girl had brought his drink before he asked the question.

"I'm looking for a girl named Taffy," he said, flipping a half-dollar onto her tray. "She's supposed to be working someplace along the street here."

"Oh, sure," the waitress replied. "I know her. But she's way down the row, and I'm right here." She pirouetted in a hip-swinging turn and leaned forward to give Longarm a good look at the cleft between her full breasts. "Do you see anything wrong with me?"

"Not a thing," Longarm assured her. "Except I got my mind set on finding Taffy."

"Anything Taffy does, I can do better," the girl said persuasively.

"Oh, this ain't nothing personal," Longarm told her. "Was I just looking for company, that'd be one thing, but I got to find this girl named Taffy to wind up some unfinished business about her family."

"Go on down about six doors, then," the girl said, her seductive tone becoming businesslike. "The place she's in is called the Red Rooster. If you feel like stopping on your way back, my name's Molly."

"I'll remember that," Longarm nodded.

Tossing off his drink, he started down the street. The Red Rooster was a virtual duplicate of the establishment he had just left: bar, gambling layouts, dance floor, small tables in the back of the building. There was also the line of idle waitresses lined up along the back wall. Instead of stopping at one of the tables, Longarm headed for the girls. They watched him expectantly as he crossed the strip of the dance floor and stopped in front of them.

"I bet one of you ladies is named Taffy," he said.

"Well, you'd just win that bet hands down, mister," one of the girls replied. She stepped forward as the others turned their heads in her direction.

Longarm sized her up quickly. Taffy was younger than he'd expected, and though her hair was blond it lacked the too-bright, brassy sheen that marked the tresses of the other three blondes in the group. The flush of rouge on her cheeks and lips made placing her age difficult. Longarm could only guess that she was somewhere between twenty-five and thirty-five. Her full breasts were puffed high by the tightly fitted bodice of her blue satin dress, and her legs thin but well formed below the knee-high hem of its skirt.

18

"What I got to talk to you about is sorta private," Longarm told her as she stopped in front of him and eyed him with a speculative frown.

"Oh, I'm sure it is," Taffy nodded. "Well, if you want a drink, we can go sit at one of the tables, or we can go right on back to my room. It's just across the alley."

"Maybe your room'd be the best place," Longarm said.

"Come on, then," she smiled, taking his hand. "If you're in that big a hurry I sure wouldn't want to keep you standing here talking." As she led him through a storeroom piled with cases of liquor and to the door that opened into the alley, Taffy went on, "I don't remember seeing you before, and I sure wouldn't forget a man as big and good-looking as you are. Who told you to ask for me, anyhow?"

"Let's wait to talk about that till we get to your room," Longarm replied. "Like I said, it's private business."

Taffy looked at him curiously, but said nothing as they crossed the narrow, trash-heaped alley and went into the building behind the saloon. Taffy led him down a hallway lined with doors and opened one of the doors near the center. The room they entered was little wider than the double bed which stood in the middle of it. The only other furniture was a straight chair and a narrow nightstand which held a washbasin and a lamp turned low.

"I guess you know business is business," Taffy told him. "I still don't know why—"

"Let's sit down, Taffy," Longarm broke in. "I got some bad news to tell you."

Her face drawn into a puzzled frown, Taffy moved around the bed and sat on its edge while Longarm settled into the chair. Her expression grew even more puzzled when, instead of beginning to talk at once, Longarm took out a cigar and lighted it. Then he produced his wallet and flipped it open to show his badge.

"I come looking for you on official business," he said. "My name's Long, Custis Long. Deputy U. S. marshal outa Denver. The first thing I got to ask you is what your

19

mother's name was before she got married."

"Yeager," Taffy replied promptly. "But she's—" She broke off abruptly and her eyes widened. "It's about Uncle Frank, isn't it? Something's happened to him? Something bad?"

"About as bad as it could be," Longarm nodded.

"He's dead. I just know he is!" Taffy said. "If he was still alive, he'd be here himself." Her eyes widened and she went on, "Did you . . ."

Longarm shook his head. "I didn't shoot him, Taffy. I was taking him to jail when the gang he'd been riding with caught up with us. That was in the north part of the Territory. I fought 'em off, and come away with a whole skin, but one of them shot your uncle. There wasn't no way I could've saved him. But before he died, he gave me something for you, and all I come here for was to hand it on to you, like I promised him I would."

Taking the watch from his pocket, Longarm passed it over to Taffy. She'd gotten over her first shock now. Her face was expressionless as she took the watch and looked at it. Then she exhaled and looked up again at Longarm.

"This was all he had, I guess?" she asked.

Longarm nodded. "I left him to be buried up at Lander," he said, standing up. "Just in case you'd want to put flowers out, or something. He had a little bit more truck, but I got to take that into my office and turn it in. Soon as the red tape's unwound, you'll be getting it. I sorta bent the rules about the watch, seeing as I promised him I'd make sure you got it."

"Well, I—I—" Taffy stammered to a stop, clenched her jaw, then went on, "Thank you, Marshal Long. I— Well, hell, you didn't want anything except to give me the watch, I guess."

"That was all," Longarm nodded.

"You're new here, aren't you, Marshal Long?" Taffy asked, her voice puzzled. "If there'd been a U. S. marshal in Rock Springs before now, I'm sure I'd've heard about it."

"Why, this ain't my station. Matter of fact, there ain't a U. S. marshal assigned to Wyoming Territory right now. I work outa the Denver office."

"And you came all this far out of your way to give me Uncle Frank's watch? Just because you'd promised him you would?"

"Well, coming down here to catch a train for Denver was just as easy as traipsing back up to Greybull."

"I suppose so," Taffy agreed, her voice still puzzled.

"Talking about traipsing, I better be getting along, now that I've handed you that watch, so I'll be bidding you good night. If you feel like you want to ask me any more questions about your uncle, I'll be staying the night at the Stockman's Hotel." He started for the door, and had his hand on the knob when Taffy spoke.

"I don't guess Uncle Frank said anything much about me, did he?" she asked. "Nothing except to give me his watch?"

"That was all," Longarm replied. "I'm sorry I had to bring you bad news, but all I set out to do was what I'd promised."

He waited for Taffy to say something else, but when she nodded and looked down again at the watch in her hand, he opened the door and went out into the alley. Following it to the street, he headed for the hotel.

Chapter 3

After his days in the saddle and the nights with nothing except a blanket between him and the sunbaked ground, the bed in Longarm's room at the Stockman's Hotel was luxuriously soft. He was sleeping soundly when the light tapping on the door aroused him. Instantly alert, as he always was on waking, he was out of the bed and padding toward the door with his Colt in his hand just as a second series of light taps sounded through its panels.

Standing well to one side of the doorframe, Longarm asked, "Who is it and what do you want?"

"It's me, Marshall Long. Taffy." Her voice was pitched just above a whisper. "You told me to come see you if I wanted to ask any more questions."

"I did, for a fact," he replied. "Wait just a second, Taffy. I ain't got anything on but my longjohns. I'll have to slip into some pants."

"Don't bother, Marshal," she said. "You're bound to know from what you saw at the Red Rooster that I've seen men in a lot less than their underwear. Go on and open the door. I won't be a bit embarrassed."

Unlocking the door, he opened it and Taffy slipped in. By the faint light trickling in through the glass transom above the door he could see that she'd thrown a hooded cloak over her shoulders but had not pulled up the hood. The feeble glow coming through the transom brought scattered gleams from her unruly blond hair, outlined her face and overly full lips, and glinted in her widened eyes.

"I'll light the lamp," he said, moving toward the bureau.

"Don't bother on my account," Taffy told him. Her eyelids fluttered as she looked around the room, letting her eyes get adjusted to its dimness. "I just wanted to ask you a little bit more about how Uncle Frank came to get killed."

"Well, sit down, then," Longarm said, indicating a chair that stood between the night-table and the bed. He moved to the table and picked up the bottle of Tom Moore. "If you'd care for a drink, to make it easier for you to talk—"

"That might help," she agreed. "I guess you know that all they let us drink at the saloon is weak tea, and I've had my fill of that. But don't bother pouring it into a glass. I don't, half the time."

Taking the bottle from Longarm, Taffy tilted it to her lips and swallowed. She handed him the bottle, then shrugged the cloak off her shoulders. Longarm sat down on the side of the bed and tilted the bottle himself. His vest hung on the bedpost and he took a cheroot from its pocket and lighted it.

In the flare of the match he could see Taffy's eyes fixed on him. He could also see that she'd thrown the cloak over the abbreviated costume she'd been wearing at the saloon. Before the match burned too short to hold, he had time to admire the bulges of her generous breasts gleaming like ivory in the yellow flame.

"What was it you was wondering about?" Longarm asked.

"You said it was one of the men in Uncle Frank's own outfit who killed him. Did they get into some kind of fight among themselves, then?"

"No, that wasn't the way of it. Your uncle had already been caught and stood trial. I was taking him to prison when three of the men outa the gang he'd been running with caught up with him."

"They're the ones who killed him? Not you?"

"It sure wasn't me, Taffy. My job was to see they didn't get him, so we fought it out. One of the gang shot him after me and him had holed up while I tried to stand 'em off."

"And he gave you the watch before he died?"

"That's about the size of it," Longarm nodded. "Was that all you wanted to know?"

"Just one more thing," Taffy replied. "You told me Uncle Frank had some more property that I'd get later. I got to wondering what it was."

"Well, it ain't such a much. It's all over there in a sack in my saddlebags. He didn't have anything but a Barlow knife and some pocket change and a few chunks of cut plug."

"Not anything like letters or papers?"

Longarm shook his head before answering quite truthfully, "That was all he had in his pockets. He'd handed me the watch just before he died, and asked me to see that you got it. If he hadn't done that, I'd've had to turn it over to the court to go in with whatever other truck he had."

Taffy sat silently for a moment, then said, "I guess my curiosity's satisfied, then. But I've got something else on my mind, Marshal. I haven't thanked you for all the trouble you took, going so far out of your way just to see that I got Uncle Frank's watch."

"Why, I was just keeping my promise," Longarm began.

Before he could finish, Taffy moved with unexpected swiftness. She covered the short distance between them with a quick step. She'd slipped one hand into the placket of his longjohns before Longarm could protest. Longarm had been without female company since leaving Denver more than a week earlier, and Taffy's expert caresses were quickly bringing him to erection. In spite of that, he made an effort.

"I didn't expect nothing from you, Taffy," he said. "All I did was pure and simple my duty to do. If you—"

24

"If I didn't enjoy what I'm doing, I wouldn't do it," she broke in. "Now just enjoy it with me."

She stood up and with one quick, long-practiced twist of her shoulders and hips slipped out of her scanty dress. Taffy pushed him on his back and straddled him, lowering herself on his rigid shaft, wriggling her hips and twisting them from side to side as she sank down to let him impale her. She stayed motionless for a moment, her head thrown back, swaying gently from side to side.

Longarm could not resist the sight of Taffy's quivering budded globes. He cradled them in his hands and caressed their buds, bringing a deep sigh from her throat. Then Taffy bent forward and started bouncing above him, groaning as their hips met each time she brought her body down.

Her movements freed her soft breasts from Longarm's hands, but when she bent further forward to twist her hips with greater freedom, the budded tips brushed across his face, and he could rub his lips over them. Taffy's body quivered when he began his new caresses, and soft moans began rising from her throat.

Longarm lay quiet for a moment, until Taffy's cries became sharper and more urgent. Then he wrapped his arms around her and held her firmly pressed to him while he rolled both of them over. When Taffy realized belatedly what he'd done in his swift move, she locked her legs around his hips as Longarm began thrusting lustily with deep plunging strokes.

Taffy writhed and groaned in pleasure as Longarm continued his deep thrusting, and when he still did not stop or slow his pace after her spasms faded and died, she lay supine for a few moments and then began squirming again, her moans of pleasure filling the small room. When at last Longarm reached his climax, she was ready to join him, and as her moans rose to a muffled shriek and her soft body writhed in frenzy he let go and jetted and sank on her with a contented sigh.

They lay in silence for several minutes. Then Taffy

stirred and Longarm rolled aside. She stepped over to the night-table and picked up the bottle of Tom Moore. Moving back to the bed, she offered it to him.

"You go ahead," Longarm told her. "I want to light me a cigar before I have a swallow."

Taffy tilted the bottle as the match Longarm struck to touch to his cigar flared and filled the room with light. Then it was dark again. In the dimness, Longarm saw Taffy stepping to the bed to hand him the bottle, saw her stumble as her feet got tangled in the clothing she'd dropped to the floor. He started to get up, but she recovered her balance quickly, gave him the bottle, and turned away, bending to pick up her dress and cloak.

Longarm had just replaced his cigar in his mouth and was drawing on it to revive the coal at its tip. As the cigar glowed he caught sight of a glint of metal in Taffy's hand in time to spring forward and grab her hand as she brought up the little whore's pistol she'd taken from some hidden pocket in her scanty skirt. She tried to free herself, but Longarm's muscular strength was far greater than hers.

"Let go of that little popgun!" he snapped.

Taffy did not obey at once, but fought against his grip until she realized her struggle was useless and released her hold on the weapon. Longarm looked at the weapon in the dim light. He'd seen such guns before, and knew how deadly they were at close range. It was even smaller than his derringer, a miniature version of his own Colt, but the wicked little pistol held five .22-caliber bullets in a cylinder only little larger in diameter than Longarm's thumb.

Tossing the pistol on the bed, he motioned for Taffy to sit down in the chair. Then he settled down on the bed and gazed at her for a moment in the dim light.

"You didn't come up here just to say thank you to me," Longarm said quietly. His voice was not accusing, but casually level. "You was after that map your uncle hid in the back of his watch. It shows where him and his partners cached away their loot, don't it?'

26

Taffy pressed her lips into a thin line and remained silent.

He continued, "He told you there'd be a map in the watch case, I imagine. Ain't that the way of it?"

"Yes, damn you!" she gasped. "That money Uncle Frank hid out at Blair's old stockade was mine! He told me I'd have it if anything happened to him! That's the only reason I've been staying in this miserable damn town, to be close to it!"

Too late Taffy realized the mistake she'd made. She pressed her hand over her mouth, her eyes widening.

"Your uncle didn't have no more right to that loot than you do, Taffy," Longarm said. "And it didn't belong to that gang, either. It's money they stole, and they killed more'n once to get their hands on it. They even killed your uncle, trying to get back the map that shows where it's hid."

Taffy made one more desperate try. "Uncle Frank said there's an awful lot of loot out there, Marshal Long," she said. "More than enough to make you and me both rich if we split it between us. Maybe if you change your mind, we could both—"

"Don't start talking about ifs and maybes," Longarm said, his voice hard, "or I'll give you a few of my own. If you don't put on your clothes and get out of here, maybe I'll take you down and put you in jail."

"But all that money!" Taffy persisted.

"It'll go back to whoever it was stolen from," Longarm told her. "There'll be a judge take care of that. Now, just be glad you're not going to jail for trying to kill me, and get outa here before I change my mind."

"So that's about the size of it, Billy," Longarm told his chief as they sat in Vail's office in the Denver federal building two days later. A dirt-crusted canvas bag, its sides bulging, lay on Vail's desk.

"And you didn't have any trouble finding where they'd put it?" the chief marshal asked.

Longarm shook his head. "Not a bit. The loot was right there where No-Nose Yeager's map showed it'd be. I'll leave it to you to turn it over to a judge and get him to figure out who it belongs to."

"I'll do that just as soon as you write your report," Vail nodded. "And I guess I ought to go over and mark a ring around today on my calendar. You finally closed a case on time, without getting into any kind of trouble."

"Now, that ain't a very nice thing for you to say, Billy," Longarm protested. "I got to admit I stretch the rules now and again, but I always try to stretch 'em in the right direction."

"I hope you haven't done too much unpacking," Vail went on. "Because another case that I'm sending you out on hit my desk yesterday evening."

"You mean you're going to send me kiting off again right away, without even giving me time to get some laundry done?"

"You won't need to worry about putting on a clean shirt for this one," Vail said. "We've got a little job to do south of the border, and our friends down there don't care how you look."

"Now, hold on, Billy!" Longarm protested. "Maybe you've forgot about it, but I sure ain't! You gave me a standing order to stay outa Mexico!"

"Which I'm changing right now," Vail said, his voice casual. "Any order I give you, I can change when I damn well please. You know that."

"I ought to. You've reminded me of it enough times."

"If I have, it's because you keep forgetting," Vail told him. "Now, what you'll be doing is going to a Rurale station where—"

"Hold up a minute, Billy!" Longarm broke in. "If I got to go messing around with the Rurales, how about you giving them Rurales an order to keep outa my way? It was you that told me they were out to get me for sure, the next time I set foot over the Rio Grande."

"It's a little bit different this time. You know damned well I wouldn't be sending you to Mexico if the Rurales were still out to get you."

"Just the same, I don't trust 'em."

"You can on this case," Vail said. "Because they're the ones asking for your help."

"Maybe you better start at the beginning," Longarm suggested. "It ain't that I doubt your word, Billy. It's just that I wouldn't trust what them Rurales said, even if they swore to it on a stack of Bibles."

"Generally, I'd agree with you," Vail said. "But you'll remember my old Rurale friend, Captain Victorio Morales?"

"Oh, sure," Longarm nodded. "Even if I did only meet him one time and didn't talk to him then much more'n five minutes."

"And you remember that Mexican outlaw the Rurales call *El Anguila del Desierto?*"

Longarm nodded. "The Desert Eel. It'd be hard to forget him. Next to the Stovespit Kid, the Eel's the slipperiest son of a bitch I ever run into."

"Well, the Rurales are pretty sure they've got him in prison down there, now," Vail went on.

"Pretty sure?" Longarm frowned. "Are you telling me they don't know?"

"That's about the size of it," Vail agreed. "And we've got an interest in making sure, too. You ought to remember why you went after the Eel in the first place."

"Oh, sure I do. He give the Rurales the slip by cutting across the Rio Grande, and robbed the post office at Del Rio to get traveling money, then stuck up the Overland Mail. I worked them cases myself, Billy, you know that."

"And brought in the Eel," Vail nodded. "Then he escaped from the court bailiff in El Paso and ducked back across the border. There's a government reward still out on him."

"I don't see why the Rurales is being so persnickety

29

about the Eel," Longarm frowned. "They still got what they call *la ley del fuego* down south of the border, or did the last time I had trouble there. And in case you been away from the border so long you've forgot, I'll tell you what that means."

Vail nodded. "Law of the gunshot. It's not something a man forgets after he's run into a few cases of it."

"I come pretty close to being tried that way myself, a time or two," Longarm reminded his chief.

"Well, they haven't exactly repealed it," Vail said. "But the Church has been bearing down pretty hard on them for being so free and easy about shooting so many of their prisoners in cold blood and then claiming they had to shoot because the prisoners were trying to escape. Besides that, the Eel's got some loot put away that I imagine the Rurales want to get their hands on."

Longarm's voice was heavy with skepticism as he asked, "You don't mean they're going by the book?"

"I wouldn't bet on it," Vail smiled. "But from what I've heard through my old Ranger friends in Texas and from the Border Patrol, the Rurales have pulled in their horns a little bit."

"You can say that all you want to, Billy. I ain't going to believe it till I see it proved."

"You'll get a chance to see for yourself, all right," Vail promised. "Because I want you to go down there and oblige Captain Morales by identifying the Eel."

"Damn it, Billy! They don't need me for that! I sure can't be the only one that can point a finger at him!"

"Morales claims you are. I had a long telegram from him day before yesterday. They're holding the Eel with some other prisoners in one of their headquarters stations, somewhere close to the border."

"Then why can't they just bring the Eel up to the border, and I'll take a look and tell 'em whether or not they got the right man?"

"There's a little more to it than that. The Eel's tucked a

lot of his loot away, and they figure him seeing you will spook him into telling them where it is. You know yourself the Eel's going to do almost anything to keep you from getting your hands on him again."

"Well, I guess if I got to go, I got to go," Longarm said resignedly. "I don't imagine I'll have too much trouble. Did Captain Morales have anything else to say?"

"As a matter of fact, he did. There'll be one of his men waiting for you at the border. He said in his letter that the best way to get there is to cross the Rio Grande at Ojinaga."

"I got a pretty good idea where that is," Longarm said thoughtfully. "I don't imagine I'll have much trouble connecting up with Morales's man."

"As far as I can see, then, there isn't anything holding you back," the chief marshal went on. "I'll tell Henry to fix up your travel orders and expense vouchers. You ought to be ready to leave tomorrow morning."

"Oh, I'll manage," Longarm said reluctantly. "But I only got one thing to tell you, Billy. This is a case I'd just as soon not be starting out on. Them damned Rurales has got memories like a bunch of elephants, and they ain't forgot that I put my fingers in their pies before. This just might be the time when the pies will be too hot, and I sure don't like the idea of my trigger finger getting sore."

Chapter 4

The conductor called "Next stop, Fort Stockton!" and the train began slowing down. Longarm looked out the window of the daycoach. The train came to a stop beside a building that looked more like an oversized tool shed than a depot. He looked beyond the tracks a quarter of a mile. Even then, his first impression was that he was seeing an unusually neat small town rather than a U. S. Army fort.

Beyond a ragged gaggle of small, shabby huts, regularly spaced adobe buildings of uniform size and shape made a tidy geometric pattern on the humped and broken ground that stretched beyond the structures to the low hills. There was no flag flying, no wall or sentry box, nothing at all military about the buildings.

Longarm picked up his rifle and saddlebags. Carrying the rifle cradled in the crook of his elbow, he swung off the train and walked up to the baggage car. One of the trainmen had already tossed his bedroll out onto the platform. The engine's whistle sounded and the train began to move again.

Longarm watched for a moment as it diminished in the distance. Then he threw the bedroll over one shoulder, balanced his rifle in one hand and his saddlebags in the other, and started walking.

The deeply rutted trace he followed was too narrow to be called a road and too wide to be called a trail, while the up-and-down country through which the train had been winding since morning was an unlikely mixture of clustered jagged hills, not high enough or big enough to be called mountains, and clearings that were not extensive enough to be described as either plains or prairies.

About the only thing around here that a man can put a proper name to is that railroad track, Longarm thought as he walked along. *It don't look like anything but what it is.*

There was neither sentry box nor sallyport, nor a flag flying to give him a hint of the location of headquarters, and no soldiers on the streets or lanes between the buildings. Longarm wandered up one of its thoroughfares and then another, between barracks and storage sheds, before he spotted the loose-hanging triangular guidon that identified the fort's headquarters.

Inside, there were no partitions separating the space into offices, just three rows of neatly aligned tables. Men in blue uniforms were working at most of them, but aside from looking up when he came in the door, they paid no attention to him. Longarm studied the insignia on their sleeves or shoulders for a moment before locating the one with the highest rank, a graying, ruddy-faced man whose shoulders bore the silver oak leaves that identified him as a lieutenant colonel.

"I guess you'd be the man I'm looking for, Colonel. I'm Custis Long, deputy U. S. marshal outa the Denver office. You're supposed to have a remount horse waiting for me here."

The officer frowned. "Name's Ransom, Long," he replied. "But I haven't heard a thing about us being expected to furnish a horse for anybody."

"Well, now," Longarm said, frowning, "that's real odd. I been three days getting here from Denver, and my boss, Chief Marshal Billy Vail, was going to send a telegram that I'd be stopping here to pick one up."

"That'd explain it, then," Ransom nodded. "We're not on the army wire any more. Some penny-squeezer back at general headquarters saw to that."

"You mean you ain't got a telegraph station here?" Longarm asked incredulously.

Ransom shook his head. "Haven't had for two years. After MacKenzie corralled the Comanches and Crook did the same for the Apaches, some bright pen-pusher in Washington got the idea that we could get along without being on the army telegraph wire. The Signal Corps took it out before we knew anything about it here, so now all the messages for us go to Fort Bliss. When they get around to it at Bliss, they send the messages here by a dispatch rider, so we're always four or five days behind."

"Seems to me like that's a hell of a way to run an army," Longarm commented. "Suppose the Mexicans was to try to take back Texas, or the Indians went on the warpath again?"

"Neither one's very likely," Ransom replied. "Besides, this place hasn't been a fighting fort since it was rebuilt right after the War. We're just a supply station, and I guess the boys at Bliss and Duncan would spread out and plug the gap if there was trouble."

"Well, I hope I won't have no trouble getting a remount horse from you, just because you didn't get the message," Longarm said. "I'm on a case down at the border, and they're looking for me to get there by tomorrow night, so I got to keep moving."

"I guess you put some time in the army during the War, Long? You look like you're old enough."

"I was just a lard-ass kid, but I got into it for a little spell before Appomattox," Longarm nodded.

"Then you'll understand about army regulations," Ransom said. "You'll just have to wait until I get the authorization. That ought to be tomorrow, next day at the latest."

"Colonel, I don't guess you understand what I just told you. I got to meet a man tomorrow night at that town called Ojinaga, and that's a real long ride from here."

"I suppose it's a Mexican you'll be meeting?" When

34

Longarm nodded, the colonel went on, "Don't worry about him, Long. He'll likely be a day late getting there."

"That's a chance I can't take, Colonel. I was aiming to stop here just long enough to pick up a horse and be right on my way. I figure I can cover a good bit of territory between now and dark, and get to Ojinaga a little bit early."

"Don't worry about having to wait a little while," Ransom said. "We'll put you up and feed you while you're waiting. All you'll be out is a little bit of time."

"Is there some regulation that keeps you from giving me a horse on your own authority?"

"I'm about three months from retirement, Marshal Long," the colonel said. "And I'm not aiming to do anything that might cost me part of my pension. But I'll tell you what. You stay here tonight. If the messenger from Bliss doesn't get here tomorrow, I'll review things in my mind and see what I can do."

"That's going to put me a day late!" Longarm protested.

Unexpectedly, the officer sitting at the next desk spoke up. "Colonel, have you thought about us being a man short for our poker game tonight? Maybe Marshal Long would feel better about staying if you invited him to sit in."

"That hadn't occurred to me, Goetz," Ransom replied. He turned back to Longarm. "I suppose you enjoy a friendly game of poker now and then?"

"I've been known to."

"Good," the colonel nodded. "Then since there's no chance that you'll be able to leave today, you're welcome to have supper at the officers' mess and join our little game."

Longarm had butted his head against the army set of mind too many times not to recognize the dead end he'd encountered now. He decided to make the best of a bad situation.

"Since it don't look like I got much choice, I guess I'll

be staying with you, and I'd sure rather be setting in on a good poker game than going to bed with the chickens," he said. "I'll just take your invitation, Colonel Ransom."

A coal-oil lamp hanging above shed a yellow glow over the table that soon after supper had been spread with a blue and white army blanket for the weekly poker game. In front of the players, stacks of gold pieces and silver dollars showed how the luck of the game, or the skill of the players, had been distributed.

At Longarm's right, Lieutenant Goetz's funds were only a little diminished. Across from Goetz, Captain Anderson had added substantially to his original stacks. Next to him, Major Douglas was in the hole a bit more than Goetz. At the end of the table, on Longarm's left, the stacks of gold and silver in front of Colonel Ransom had shrunk very substantially. Longarm, playing conservatively, had been the heavy winner. Most of the losses of his fellow players had swelled his stakes at one time or another as the evening wore on.

"I'd say we'd better make this the last hand," Ransom said as he gathered the cards and squared them. "The mess squad will be coming in to start breakfast pretty soon, now."

"Being the heavy loser doesn't influence your suggestion, does it, Jack?" Anderson asked, chuckling.

"Not a bit," the commander replied quickly. "I intend to get even at least on this hand."

"We'll all be keeping an eye on you after that remark," Douglas said.

"I don't think you can do it," Anderson went on. He took a gold eagle from the stack in front of him and pushed it toward Ransom. "If you're so sure, how about a little side bet, high man between you and me?"

Ransom shook his head. "No, thanks. I'll settle for what I take in the pot."

"I'll take your bet, Bob," Goetz said. He shoved a coin

out to join the gold piece the captain had offered.

Longarm watched the byplay in silence. From the beginning of supper at the officers' table he'd been aware of his status as an outsider. His companions had been friendly enough, but at the same time their conversation, dealing with events at the post, and their personal joking had tended to exclude him. He sat silent now as Ransom divided the deck and began shuffling.

Over the faint rustling rattle of the cards he was shuffling, the post commander said, "We'll make this an honest game. Five-card stud. I've got to take a few dollars from you fellows on every card I deal, just to get even."

"If you expect to do that, we'd better take off the limit, too," Major Douglas suggested.

"That suits me," Ransom nodded. He looked around the table and, when no one objected, said, "No limit and no checking, then."

His next shuffle finished, Ransom squared the deck again and shoved it toward Longarm to cut. Picking up the cards, he waited for the players to ante, then dealt a card facedown and followed the deal quickly with a second card, this one faceup.

Only Goetz and Ransom had looked at their hole cards. Longarm did not look at his now, but watched the other players as they peered covertly at theirs. None of them changed expression after they had looked, but all of them glanced around the table to check the cards lying faceup.

Longarm was doing the same thing. His own card was a nine of diamonds. Goetz had gotten the diamond deuce, Ransom a seven of clubs, Douglas the queen of clubs, Anderson a six of hearts. Now Longarm slid a horn-hard thumbnail under one corner of his hole card and saw it was the diamond queen.

"Your queen bets, Doug," Ransom said, just as the major slid a silver cartwheel into the center of the table.

Without waiting for the other players to toss their bets into the pot, Ransom picked up the deck and started dealing again. A second queen, hearts this time, fell to Douglas. Anderson received another six, Goetz the five of clubs, Longarm threw the eight of diamonds. Ransom dealt himself the spade trey.

"Your bet again, Doug," the colonel announced.

"Since it's the last round, my pair of queens ought to be worth five dollars," the major said.

He flipped a half-eagle into the pot, and without comment the others met his bet. Longarm had started reaching for his hole card when Ransom resumed dealing. This time Douglas got a club deuce, Anderson a nine of spades, Goetz the diamond six, and Longarm another diamond, this time the ten. Ransom dealt himself another seven, hearts.

"Your pair of queens are still high, Doug," Ransom announced. "How much is it going to cost us to stay?"

"I'll let you get off easy," the major replied. "Ten."

There was the soft clinking of coins falling on top of those already in the pot as all five of the players stayed. Colonel Ransom picked up the deck to deal the final cards. He dropped the deuce of diamonds on the table in front of Douglas.

"Well, now," the major smiled. "Two nice pairs."

Ransom flipped a card to the captain, the spade six. Anderson allowed himself a smile, then said, "There's a lot of power on the table. Too much for my pair of sixes to hold up."

By this time the colonel had dealt Goetz the five of clubs.

"Looks like I'm in the soup," the lieutenant commented. He watched as Ransom dealt Longarm the jack of diamonds, and added, "Marshal Long might be sitting on something good, though."

Longarm sat silently, waiting for Ransom to deal himself the final card. The colonel dropped the trey of clubs on the table to round out his own hand, then looked at his cards silently for a moment before putting aside what remained of the deck.

"Your queen-high pair bets," he told Douglas.

"I'll have to see what you fellows do," Douglas commented. "But I'll make it easy for you. If you want to see my hole card it'll only cost you twenty."

"Sound like you're sitting on a good one," Anderson said, then tossed a double eagle on the heap of coins in the center of the table. "But I've got twenty dollars' worth of curiosity."

"I'd be a fool to stay in," Goetz commented, sweeping his cards up and tossing them on the deck. "But this ought to be pretty interesting to watch."

"I can't stay interested without a stake in the game," Longarm told them. "I'll call."

"That's not good enough," Ransom announced. He laid an eagle and a double eagle on the heap of coins. "It's going to cost you ten more than that, Marshal Long."

"Well, I'm in for so much now that I got to go along for the ride," Longarm said, adding an eagle to his earlier bet.

Ransom looked at Douglas and asked, "Are you seeing, raising, or folding?"

"Give me a minute to figure it out," the major replied. He scanned the table quickly, and went on, "My guess is that one of you're bound to be bluffing. I'll see this one, just in case I'm guessing right."

"Somebody's sure sitting on a real hand," Anderson frowned. He studied the cards in front of each player as he went on, "The diamond seven's not up, neither is the queen, so the marshal could have us all beat, but he could be bluffing. Jack, unless you've got a trey or a seven, I've got you beat on the table. Doug, I think you and the marshal are both running a bluff, and if you are . . ." He took two double eagles from their stack and laid them carefully on the growing pot. "I guess I'm fool enough to pay to find out."

Ransom looked at Longarm and asked, "How about it, Marshal Long? Who's outbluffing who?"

"Oh, I wouldn't make a guess," Longarm said levelly.

"But, like I said before, I'll go along for the ride." His face as expressionless as his voice, he added another eagle to the stakes. "It'll be interesting to see who's man enough to ride with me."

"I sure as hell will!" Ransom snapped. "I don't believe your hole card's all that good, not with three sixes and three queens showing."

There was now almost $250 in the pot. Ransom's earlier bets had reduced his pile of coins to a mere half-dozen eagles. He flicked them with his forefinger, frowning, then pushed the stack into the pot. "Will you two call my sixty?"

Major Douglas had laid his cards facedown on the table after his last bet. He looked from the cards to the swollen pot and finally tossed his hand on the discard pile, saying, "I hate to take a loss, but I think I'll let Marshal Long fight it out with you, Jack."

"It's up to you, then, Long," Ransom said.

"Oh, I ain't about to fold," Longarm said. "But I wonder if you'd be interested in a little side bet, Colonel?"

"What kind of side bet?" Ransom frowned. "I won't have any money left to cover a bet until next payday."

"Money's not what I got in mind," Longarm replied. "I was thinking about the fix I'm in, waiting here till you get that mailbag from Fort Bliss." He draw his Colt and laid it on the table. "Now, that's as fine-tuned a weapon as you'll find anyplace. I'll put it up against your word that if you lose you'll save me the waiting I'd have to do till you get the word about letting me have a horse and saddle gear."

Ransom's frown grew deeper. "That's a fine weapon, Long. I'd imagine you set a good deal of store by it."

"I do," Longarm agreed.

"But if you win, I'd have to break a standing order," the colonel said thoughtfully.

Longarm's offer of the unusual bet had drawn the fascinated attention of the other players. They were not bothering to conceal their interest, waiting for Ransom to make up his mind. Finally Major Douglas spoke.

"Every one of us will guarantee to keep our mouths shut if you take the marshal's bet, Jack," he said.

"That's right," Anderson and Goetz agreed, speaking almost in unison.

Then Anderson added, "It's a sporting proposition, Colonel. Are you going to let the U. S. Marshal's force bluff the army into backing down?"

In that moment, the bet Longarm had proposed moved from the status of one poker player against another to a contest between the two services. Studying his opponent's face, Longarm saw the colonel move from irresolution to resolve.

"I guess that's what it comes down to, all right," Ransom said slowly. "Damned if I'm not going to take you up on it, Long." He paused for a moment, then continued, "I'll even go you one better and sweeten my bet a little bit. If I bust out, I'll get the hostlers out of their bunks and see you on the trail tonight, if you want to push on right away."

"Well, I got to admit I had that in mind," Longarm said. "Have we got a bet, then?"

"We sure as hell have!" Ransom agreed. "Let's turn our cards up and see which one of us is the winner!"

Looking one another in the eye, the bettors reached for their hole cards. Almost simultaneously, they reached for the cards that still lay facedown, but Ransom turned his up a second or two before Longarm exposed his.

When the other officers saw that Ransom's hole card was a seven, they began smiling. Then Longarm exposed his queen of diamonds and their smiles vanished.

"Looks like my straight flush takes your full house, Colonel," Longarm said quietly.

"Damn it! I was dead sure you were bluffing!" Ransom exclaimed. "With that six of diamonds showing in the captain's hand, I didn't see how in hell you could've filled

41

out. I guess I didn't give you enough credit. I ought've known you wouldn't bet the way you did if you hadn't been holding the cards."

"When you kept raising, I was right glad I did," Longarm smiled. "No hard feelings, is there?"

"Hell, no!" Ransom replied. "You proved you were a better poker player, and I don't suppose there's one of us here that would carry a grudge against a man just because he knew how to play out his hand."

"Well, I might not've pushed hard as I did if I didn't have to get to where I'm headed on time," Longarm admitted. "But I wasn't joking you when I said I had to be in Ojinaga by tomorrow night, so I sure didn't stop pushing my luck when I seen I had a chance to get there on time."

"Even if you start at daylight, you'll never make it in a day," the major frowned.

"I wasn't planning to wait till daylight." Turning to Ransom, Longarm went on, "What would you do, Colonel, if you got an order at this time of night to meet up with bunch of your men that was going to be in bad trouble if you didn't get to 'em by daybreak?"

"Why, I'd have a horse saddled up and—" Ransom stopped short and nodded. "I see what you're driving at, Long. We'll get you on your way without holding you up any longer." Turning to Goetz, he said, "Roust up a couple of men, Lieutenant, and tell them to put a good saddle on that chestnut that came in last week. And tell them I want to see the horse saddled and ready and here in front of the mess hall in fifteen minutes!"

Chapter 5

A gibbous moon hanging low in the sky provided almost enough light for Longarm to make out details of the starkly barren landscape. The air was still except for the faint rustlings of lizards scuttling off the trail ahead of his horse and the occasional eerie yowl of a distant coyote.

By the time daylight arrived, he had reached the last of the broken hills that stretched away from the great Bandera Mesa. On the gentle downslope he could make better time than was possible through the broken, gullied mesaland over which he'd been traveling since leaving Fort Stockton.

Although the going was smoother, it seemed to Longarm that he was almost standing still. The unchanging character of the land surrounding him offered few landmarks by which to judge his progress. Even with his years of travel over most of the West, Longarm still had the difficulty experienced by all Western travelers in estimating distances by the line of the horizon above the slow arc of the blazing sun that inched across the sky, casting his shadow ahead of him.

By this time Longarm was silently swearing at himself for having been in such a hurry to leave after the poker game. There were only two small pieces of jerky and half a hardtack biscuit in his saddlebag, and though his canteen was half-full, the water was stale.

In spite of his growing hunger, Longarm delayed eating

for as long as he could. When the sun was directly over-head, he stopped for a few minutes and dismounted. He nibbled at the jerky and hardtack while he paced back and forth to stretch his long legs and let the horse breathe.

Stopping did nothing to temper his urge to get on to the end of his journey. As soon as he judged that the horse had rested enough, he washed down the jerky and hardtack with a swallow of Tom Moore from the bottle in his saddle-bag, then levered himself into the saddle again and started moving.

When he was faced with the need to cover long dis-tances on a horse across featureless terrain, Longarm had fallen into the habit of using his time to plan. He did so now, in silent conversation with himself as the cavalry mount plodded steadily ahead.

Billy Vail worked in this border country with the Texas Rangers for a long enough time to know what the Rurales is like, his thoughts ran. *But Billy's been away from here too many years to remember how tricky them bastards can be. They never give up on a man that's beat 'em to the draw as many times as you have, old son. So you better stay awake as long as you can, and then sleep with one eye open when you doze off.*

Now, was I wearing one of them big fancy gold-threaded hats the Rurales favors, I'd figure out a way to pull a man I want down into Mexico, and aim to get my hands on him just as soon as he wades across the Rio Grande. And I'd have somebody watching for him on the American side of the river, to keep an eye on him and see did he have company, somebody to cover his back. So the best way to get the Rurales off-balance, if they got men out looking for you, is to come up behind 'em. That'd spoil whatever plans they might've made, and give you time to figure out your own move.

Glancing up at the sun, now dipping into its downward slide toward the western horizon, Longarm twitched the reins to turn his horse and started at a long slant that would bring him to the Rio Grande a few miles upriver from the town of Ojinaga.

When Longarm at last reached the river, there was still a faint line of light outlining the distant peaks of the Sierra Madre del Norte. This was the long spine of mountains that stretched from the wide northernmost part of Mexico to the narrow isthmus it became far to the south. The greatest and highest peaks of the range were far distant, but the foothills extended almost to the Rio Grande.

Following the river until he found a place where the unmistakable sheen of the surface marked a sandy shoaling bottom, Longarm splashed across to the Mexican side just as the last line of light disappeared from the western sky. As darkness deepened, he could see the lights of Ojinaga to his left, a half-dozen miles downstream. He headed toward them, easing up on his tired horse now that his destination was in sight.

A half-hour more of travel, the tired remount horse now plodding ahead at a walk and moving with increasing reluctance, brought him to the outskirts of Ojinaga. The town was little more than a line of shanties, three or four deep, along the dirt road to the river.

Darkness had settled in fully by now, and except for a bright patch of lights at the wagon bridge across the Rio Grande, the only illumination was the rectangles of yellow lampglow that spilled from the windows of the small houses that stood on each side of the road. A dozen yards from the bridge, Longarm reined in and settled back in his saddle, looking at the wooden span and the handful of loungers around the little wooden sentry box that housed the customs inspector.

He spotted the Rurale immediately, by the glint of gold threads in the ornamental design that almost hid the black felt of his sombrero. A hitch-rail stood between Longarm and the Rurale and he toed his mount up to it. Swinging

45

out of the saddle, he walked up to the Rurale.

"You'd be looking for somebody from across the river, I guess?" he asked the man.

For a moment after he'd turned to face Longarm, the Rurale did not reply. Then he said curtly, "What I look for ees no affair of yours."

Relieved that the man spoke English, Longarm replied, "It is if I'm the one you're waiting for."

"You are the American *Policia Federal?*" the Rurale asked, gesturing toward the United States side of the river.

"Now, if I wasn't, how'd I know to look for you here?"

Longarm's logic seemed to disconcert the Rurale, who thought about the question for several moments before replying. *"Es verdad,"* he nodded. "You have the badge to show me, no?"

Longarm took out his wallet and flipped it open to display his marshal's badge. The Rurale bent close to inspect it, then scanned Longarm's face again.

"Bueno," he finally said. *"Se habla Español?"*

Longarm shook his head. "I know just enough to understand what you asked me, but that's about all."

"No es importante. I am speak the Eenglish very good. We weel talk in eet, then. I am Eulario Gomez, *sergente de los Rurales."*

"My name's Long, Custis Long."

Neither Longarm nor Gomez offered to shake hands.

"You are to meet me here," Gomez went on. "But I am to take you to someone else, no? You weel please geev me hees name, so I am sure you are who you say."

"You're going to take me to wherever I'll find Captain Victorio Morales."

Gomez nodded and said, *"Es bueno.* We weel start at once."

"Not on your life we won't!" Longarm told him firmly. I been in the saddle since before daylight, and I ain't had a square meal since supper last night. If we're heading some-

46

place else, I got to have a bit to eat first."

"Ojinaga ees a small place," Gomez replied. "Ees no *ristorante,* only one leetle cantina, but they weel sell you tamales and tacos eef you buy *cerveza.*"

"That's better'n hardtack and jerky," Longarm said. "Can we lead our horses to this place? I'd like to give my legs a good stretch out before we start for whatever place it is you're supposed to take me."

"Een Ojinaga, everytheeng ees close," Gomez smiled. "Come weeth me. I weel show you. Ees not far."

The Rurale started away from the area of lighted dwellings that clustered around the bridge. The street dwindled to a narrow road, little more than a lane, and the houses bordering it stood farther apart. They had gone a bit less than a quarter of a mile when his companion stopped in front of a house which, unlike those around it, had an open door.

"Ees safe to leave here the horses," Gomez said. "And we weel be inside for only a leetle time."

Longarm followed the Rurale into a low-ceilinged room. A lantern dangling from a wire attached to one of the low ceiling beams provided an uncertain light. For the first time, Longarm got a look at his companion.

Gomez's head barely reached to Longarm's shoulder, but the gold-embroidered peaked hat he wore made him seem taller. He had on a *charro* jacket, also richly embroidered, a stained white shirt and flare-legged trousers. A holstered Colt dangled from his hip. His face was what in Mexico had come to be called *tipo Benito Juarez,* the broad, heavy jaw and square face with high cheekbones that told of Indian ancestry. He was clean-shaven, but badly in need now of a shave.

Longarm's gaze swept the room. It was furnished with three or four tables, all unoccupied. A bar made by resting a plank across beer kegs stretched along the side wall. A low door in the center of the opposite wall led to a second

47

room. In it there were two unpainted tables, chairs, and a homemade sheet-iron stove, nothing more than a box fitted with a stovepipe, which stood in a corner.

An immensely fat woman sat near the stove. She struggled to her feet as Longarm and the Rurale entered. Looking at Gomez, she said, *"Que tal?"*

"Quieremos comer," the Rurale replied. *"Que haces?"*

"Tacos y tamales," she shrugged. *"No hay chili verde ni mole. Que quieres?"*

Longarm had been south of the border often enough to get the drift of her reply. He said, "Tacos and tamales will be fine, *señorita*. About six of each of 'em."

"Y cerveza," Gomez added.

By the time Longarm had munched through half a dozen of the hot, crisp tacos and an equal number of the cornhusk-wrapped tamales, his stomach no longer complained. After one swallow, he'd refused to drink the warm Mexican beer, but had kept his guide adequately supplied.

As he leaned back in his chair and lighted a cigar, Longarm said to Gomez, "Well, that wasn't much like meat and potatoes, but it'll hold me for a while. Whenever you're ready to ride, I'm with you."

"Then ees best we go now," Gomez nodded. "Eet weel be late when we get to where *el Capitan* ees waiteeng." As they walked toward the door, he started to say something more, hesitated for a moment, then asked, "I am curious about one theeng, Marshal Long. Why you are not come across the breedge?"

"You oughta be able to figure that out, Gomez. I been down here in Mexico before, and news has a way of getting out when a private deal like the one I'm on is being fixed up. Now, I sure didn't want to get shot off my horse while I was halfway across that bridge over yonder. So I just waded the river a little ways upstream and come at you from behind."

"Eh!" Gomez exclaimed. "You are theenk like a Rurale!"

"I guess you aimed that to be a compliment, so that's how I'll take it," Longarm said. "But it's getting late. We better start moving. Just give me time to get a few cigars outa my saddlebag."

As Longarm stepped past Gomez toward the horses, a shot broke the night's stillness. Gomez cried out and dropped. Longarm hit the ground a split-second later, his Colt already in his hand, his eyes searching the area from which the shot had come.

Since he hadn't been looking directly at the spot, all that he had to go by was the memory of a half-seen spurt of muzzle-blast. Now he saw no point in giving away his position to the hidden sniper, though he was not sure whether the ambusher's target was himself or Gomez. Behind him the Rurale was moaning softly.

"You hit, Gomez?" Longarm asked without turning his head.

Sí. But ees only scratch. You see nobody in dark, no?"

"No. And I didn't get a good look at the muzzle-flash. You think whoever's after us is still out there?"

"Como sí, como no," the Rurale replied.

His tone gave Longarm the feeling that Gomez, like himself, had been shot at so many times that the experience was no novelty any longer. The Rurale was holding his right hand clamped over his left shoulder, and his left hand was dangling limply at his side.

"I better take a look at the bullet hole you got there," Longarm suggested.

"Better I keep tight hold like I do now, so I do not lose much blood. Like I tell you, ees only scratch."

"Can you still handle a gun?" he asked the Rurale.

"Sí, a pistola. No puedo anaje mi fusil."

"A rifle wouldn't help you none," Longarm told him. "Whoever that bushwhacker is, we'd've heard him if he run away, so chances are he's still in pistol range. I got a feeling he's waiting out there someplace. He likely figures we'll move around and give him a target."

49

"Creo que es verdad," Gomez replied. *"Pues, que hacemos ahorita?"*

Longarm's understanding of Spanish exceeded his ability to speak it. He said, "There ain't a hell of a lot we can do till we flush out that damn sniper. For all we know, he's still over there someplace, waiting for another chance at us. You stay here and keep your head down. I'll belly-crawl over in the direction that shot come from and see what I can stir up. Just don't get careless and take a shot in my direction, even if I start shooting."

Preoccupied with the unexpected bushwhacker, Longarm had not been aware of the sudden change that had taken place along the street during the few moments that followed the gunfire. On both sides of the narrow unpaved road, the lighted windows that had shed their glow on its gravel surface were now dark. The cantina where they'd eaten was now blacked out as completely as the houses on both sides of it. Not a sound broke the eerie silence.

For the first few yards he covered as he moved away from the Rurale, Longarm crawled. He did not try to hurry, but inched along, trying to pierce the inky blackness ahead of him. He saw nothing, even though his night vision had returned by now, and while he strained to hear any noise from the darkness ahead, there was none.

That son of a bitch is either cagey enough to keep still, or he's long gone, old son, he told himself as he stopped to listen. *And you're stirring up enough noise trying to make like you're a snake so that he could take a sound-shot and come close enough to hitting you to make no never-mind*.

As though the unseen adversary had read Longarm's thoughts, a rifle shot broke the stillness ahead and a bullet plowing into the ground inches from him sent a shower of loose dirt and gravel into Longarm's face.

Through the dustup of the bullet he saw the muzzle-flash of the sniper's rifle, a crimson streak etched for a fleeting second in the darkness ahead. Longarm answered it with a shot from the Winchester, aiming at the place where the muzzle-blast had spurted red in the blackness.

Levering fresh shells in the chamber with the speed gained by long experience, he bracketed the spot with shots on each side of his first aiming point, then rolled aside. A split-second after he'd moved, the shooter hidden by the darkness let off a shot in reply. The menacing whine of a slug sounded above his head and grated into the hard ground behind him with a solid thunk.

Longarm leaped up and began running in a low crouch toward the spot where the spurt of flame had shown the mystery sniper to be. He tried once more to pierce the darkness with his eyes, and failed as thoroughly as he had before. Then, over the scraping of his own bootsoles on the hard ground, he heard hoofbeats from the darkness ahead and knew that the gunman had given up and was retreating.

Longarm held his ground for a moment longer, trying to fix the position of the hoofbeats and the direction the horse was taking. He waited until the thuds had grown almost inaudible before giving up and turning to grope his way through the night to the spot where he'd left Gomez.

A call from the Rurale guided him. "Here, Marshal Long! *Un poco mas al derecho!*" As Longarm drew closer, Gomez asked, "Ees no good, yes?"

"Not a damn bit of good," Longarm replied.

The Rurale's right hand was still closed tightly over his left shoulder.

"It'd have been just plain luck if I'd hit whoever it was," Longarm went on. "You got any idea who might've been doing that shooting?"

"No way to know. But ees not strange. Many people do not like Rurales. Ees same, from your country, no?"

"Oh, I guess we got our share," Longarm said. "How bad are you hurt?"

"Ees not bad," the Rurale said. "Not good, but ees almost stop to bleed."

"That wound's not going to heal up if we're going to do some fast riding tonight," Longarm said. "You better let

51

me see what I can do for you."

"Here een dark, weeth notheeng for *vendaje,* what ees eet you can do?"

"I got a spare bandanna in my saddlebag," Longarm offered. "And it wouldn't be the first time I've tied up a bullet-crease without much light."

"Eet weel be all right!" Gomez insisted stubbornly.

"Wait a minute!" Longarm exclaimed. "How about that place where we had supper? Will them folks let us in where we can see? Maybe the lady could put on some kind of bandage, so that crease won't open up and start bleeding again when we move on."

"*Creo que sí,*" Gomez answered. "We try."

After several minutes of prolonged knocking at the door of the cafe, the woman's voice called from within. "*Quien es?*"

"Gomez," the Rurale replied. "*Soy herido. Requime ropa para faja.*"

"*Momentito,*" she replied. The sound of a match scraping came through the half-open door, then its flame flared inside and the yellow glow of lantern light appeared. The woman opened the door wider to allow Longarm and Gomez to enter. When she saw Gomez holding his shoulder, she exclaimed, "*Ay de mi! 'Sta herida?*"

"*Un poco garrapate,*" Gomez replied.

"*Se nesecita agua caliente y paño,*" she told Gomez. "*Venga conmigo. Andale!*"

"Maybe so you bring horses," Gomez told Longarm before he turned to follow the woman into the other room. "Eet weel take leetle time to feex my shoulder. Then we ride on."

Longarm nodded and groped his way back to the horses. Before returning to the cantina, he dipped into his saddlebag and reloaded his rifle. Then he led the horses back with him, guided by the light from the open door. Just as he entered the place, Gomez came through the door of the other room, his left shoulder swathed with a thick layer of cloth that had been wrapped around his upper arm and shoulder over his jacket.

"You all right?" Longarm asked.

"*Tal bueno,*" the Rurale shrugged. He winced as his shoulder moved. "Ees all right. We go now."

"Well, that sure don't look like much of a bandaging job to me," Longarm told him. "But you know how you feel better'n I do. Come on, let's mount up and ride."

Chapter 6

Longarm and Gomez rode through the darkness. After they had covered what Longarm estimated to be six or eight miles, the Rurale began swaying in his saddle and moaning now and then. His groans were loud enough for Longarm to hear them over the horses' hoofbeats.

"Sounds to me like you ain't feeling so good," Longarm said. "You figure you can make it the rest of the way?"

"I am not feel good," Gomez replied. "But I weel not geeve up. And we are to be there *poco a poco.*"

After they had traveled another mile or two, Gomez turned his horse off the road onto a track that was almost invisible in the darkness. When Longarm finally succeeded in following it with his eyes, he could see that the ghostly trace ran over the brow of a ridge that lay just ahead of them. They mounted the ridge. Beyond its crest, the ground fell away into a rounded valley. In the bottom of the depression, showing dimly in the darkness, Longarm could make out the night-ghosted bulk of a large building.

"Is this the place we're headed for?" he asked.

"*Sí.* Here we stop."

"Hold on now!" Longarm said sharply. He reined in his horse. Gomez pulled up also and turned to face Longarm.

"What ees wrong?" he asked.

"I ain't sure I like what I've got into," Longarm replied.

"You say you do not trust me?" Gomez asked.

"It ain't that, Gomez. Maybe I just didn't understand

you a while ago when you said we had a long ride. This ain't more'n a hop, skip, and jump from Ojinaga."

Gomez was silent for a moment. Then, with great dignity in his voice, he replied, *"Señor Long, in my shoulder ees bullet wound I get when I try to keep you safe. Do you theenk I am do thees from some plan that ees breeng you to harm?"*

Longarm shook his head. "I'm sorry, Gomez. What I said sounded a lot worse than I meant it to. But I had a couple of run-ins with your outfit before, and after that little shooting scrape we got mixed up in a while ago, I guess I'm still sorta edgy."

"Thees I am onderstan," the Rurale nodded. "But you weel see what you weel see."

"All right," Longarm nodded. "Let's go on."

Gomez turned his horse and started toward the building. Longarm followed. As they drew closer, the *hacienda* looked more and more impressive. Behind the big main house, Longarm could see lights glowing from small huts. In their glow he saw that beyond the huts there were pens for horses and cattle.

Gomez reined in at the massive front door and dismounted. When he motioned for Longarm to follow suit, Longarm swung out of the saddle and joined him. A huge iron knocker was mounted on the door, and Gomez rapped loudly, three bangs, a pause, then three more.

A light showed in a window on one side of the door, and in a moment the door swung open. An immensely fat man stood in the opening. He carried a double-barreled shotgun cradled in the crook of his elbow. His bulk almost totally hid the much smaller man who stood behind him holding a candlestick aloft.

Gomez said quickly, *"Es tan bueno, jefe. Mira! Tenemos Marshal Long, antes que puede hablar con Capitan Morales."*

"De seguro!" the fat man wheezed. His voice was low, almost a whisper, and Longarm was still trying to puzzle

55

out what Gomez had said when the man jerked up the barrel of the shotgun and shoved its muzzle into Longarm's midsection. In almost unaccented English, he said, "We have been waiting for you, Marshal Long. You will stand very quietly while your bite is removed. Gomez, take his pistol!"

Longarm had no choice but to stand motionless while Gomez slid his Colt from its holster.

"No tiene otra pistola?" the man asked Gomez. *"He buscale?"*

Gomez hesitated for only a fraction of a second before replying. *"No tiene otra pistola, jefe. Un fusil a su caballo, no mas."*

"Pues, su herido postizo enganate?" the fat man asked.

"Completamente." The Rurale grinned. "Long *nunca tiene una pizca."*

As he spoke, Gomez tugged at the bandage that swathed his shoulder. When it fell away, his jacket showed no signs of blood or a bullet hole. Longarm knew then how thoroughly he'd been tricked. A frown grew on his face as he realized the reason for the elaborate charade that had put him in his present uncomfortable situation.

"Pone la candelaria sobre la mesa, Ramirez," the fat man said over his shoulder. *"Y despues encagarse los caballos."*

Turning away from the fat man, the one holding the lighted candelabra moved to set the candlestick on the table. When he turned back and started through the door to attend the horses, Longarm could see him clearly for the first time. He recognized him at once as the proprietor of the cantina where he and Gomez had stopped.

By now, Longarm had worked out each step of the elaborate imposture that had brought him to his present situation. There was only one course he could see to follow, and he saw no use in wasting time to lay the groundwork. Ignoring the threat of the shotgun's muzzle pressing into his stomach, he turned his head to face the Rurale.

56

"I guess I got to hand it to you, Gomez," he said. "You done a real good job of playing me for a fool. That fake bandage taken me in pretty smart, but you acted so much like a real Rurale that I didn't even think about asking you to show your badge and prove you was."

Contempt in his voice, Gomez replied, "Eef you have ask me I would show you my badge. Eet would be the same, Long. I am a real Rurale."

"Then what the hell is all this about?" Longarm asked. He looked back at the fat man. "I guess the next thing I'll find out is that you're a Rurale, too."

"Not at the moment," the man said. He stepped to one side, but kept the shotgun muzzle pressed into Longarm's midriff. "We will go into the *sala* and be seated so we can talk comfortably. I have been standing too long. Gomez, guard our friend the marshal."

Gomez jabbed Longarm's Colt into his back and said, "Make no foolish moves, Long. Do as *el jefe* say."

"Don't worry, Gomez," Longarm replied over his shoulder as he started following the fat man down the wide corridor. "I ain't a complete fool, even if I acted like one for a little while."

Leading the way into a luxuriously furnished room off the hall, the fat man lighted a lamp. Just as its light brightened the room, a massive clock in one corner began chiming. Longarm was surprised when the mellow tone of the striker stopped at ten. He realized with some surprise that not quite four hours had passed since his arrival at Ojinaga.

A gesture of the fat man's hand caught his eye, and Longarm sat down in the chair he had indicated. The fat man dropped with a sigh of relief onto a sofa. Gomez stationed himself behind Longarm, holding the Colt's cold muzzle against the back of his neck.

For a moment, the fat man gazed thoughtfully at Longarm. Then he said, "There has been no time for me to introduce myself, Long. I am Don Claudio Calderon. You may have heard my name before."

57

Longarm nodded. "Seems like I have, but I ain't heard it lately. I sorta had an idea you was dead."

"As you can see, I am very much alive. But your name is one I know well. You embarrassed me several times when it was my privilege to serve as *comandante* of the Rurales until the bastard *Indio* Diaz seized power for a second term as president."

"I can figure out the rest of it for myself," Longarm broke in. "You got mad because Diaz fired you, and now you've got up a scheme of some kind to get rid of him so you can put in somebody who'll give your old job back to you."

"You surprise me, Long," Calderon said. "In your crude language, you have stated the situation very clearly. There is much more to it than you understand, of course, but you will learn about those things very soon." Turning to Gomez, he asked, "Has he told you anything yet that will help us?"

Gomez shook his head. "I have not time for ask questions, *jefe*. I am remember the danger you are warn me about, and move weeth much speed."

Calderon nodded. "*Seguro*. We have less time now, but if we can persuade Marshal Long to see the justice of our cause, perhaps he will help us."

"Don't count on it, Calderon," Longarm broke in. "I was sent here to do a job, and I aim to finish it."

With a twisted smile, Calderon said, "I admire your spirit, Long. But I should not need to remind you that you are not able to correct your present situation. Your life is in my hands. Whether I give it back to you will depend on how you respond to my offer."

"I ain't heard you offer anything yet," Longarm replied.

His voice hardening, the fat man said, "For one thing, I can keep you alive or I can tell Gomez to kill you. Life in my country is very cheap."

"Oh, I noticed that, the few times I been here," Longarm nodded. "And I got a pretty good notion that if you was to tell Gomez to pull the trigger of that sixgun he's poking in my neck, he'd do it in a minute."

"You make only one error in your assumption, Long." Calderon smiled, his lips twisted nastily.

"What's that?"

"I would not order Gomez to shoot you in this room. I don't suppose you would understand that the Kurdistan carpet on the floor—a very fine example, by the way—is worth far more to me than your life. I would not ruin it with bloodstains."

"Well, now, you've had your little joke, Calderon," Longarm said calmly. "Suppose you tell me what you got in mind?"

"I want the loot which the man who calls himself *El Anguila del Desierto* has hidden in your country," Calderon replied.

"You sure do know a lot about my business." Longarm frowned thoughtfully. "It seems to me like you know more about the job I was sent here for than I do myself. Mind telling me how you come to find out so much?"

Calderon shrugged. "Diaz is not a popular president, and I have many ears in the Rurales, men who served under my command and who are still loyal to me."

"Like Gomez, I guess?"

"Correct. But a revolution is very expensive. I have already spent a great deal of money on the one which I have started. A great deal more is needed if I am to succeed."

"I guess I can figure it all out now," Longarm said. "If you can beat Diaz's men to where the Eel's cached his loot, you'd come up with a pretty good-sized chunk of cash that'd help pay for your revolution."

"A shrewd observation," Calderon said. "And since I know your reputation in your own country, I will tell you openly that you are a man whose services I can use."

Longarm shook his head. "I got one job already. Even if I was interested in a proposition from you—which I ain't —I'm going to finish what I come here to do."

"Big talk will get you nothing!" Calderon snorted. "But the hour is late, and your day has been very busy. Perhaps when you have slept, you will be able to see things more clearly." He turned to Gomez. "Eulario, take him to the safe room. We will leave him there until tomorrow. Then I will talk with him again."

Gomez prodded Longarm with the Colt's muzzle. Longarm stood up and turned around. Gomez indicated the door with the hand in which he held the Colt. Longarm walked into the hall without protest. He realized that now he faced the need to plan and to bide his time until he'd worked out a scheme that would get him free.

Gomez pointed to the staircase, and followed close behind Longarm as he went up the steps. When Longarm stopped on the second-floor landing, Gomez shook his head and gestured for him to go up the next flight. There was no carpeting on the steps leading to the third floor, nor was there any on the long corridor that extended the length of the building. Gomez indicated a door a few feet from the landing, and when Longarm reached it, the Rurale spoke for the first time.

"Do not meestake *el jefe's* kind treatment," he warned. "Eef you do not leesten to heem tomorrow, he weel order me to keel you." Prodding the muzzle of the Colt into Longarm's back, Gomez reached past him and removed the metal peg from the heavy hasp on the door. Longarm stepped inside. Gomez reached for the door handle, hesitated for a moment, and added, "And I weel do as he tells me."

"I ain't making no mistake about that," Longarm said, his voice casual. "But tomorrow's a long ways off, and I got plenty of time to think about what your boss said." He held up his hand as Gomez started to close the door. "Oh, you might tell the cook, I like two fried eggs for breakfast."

Gomez's jaw dropped and his eyes widened. He started to say something, thought better of it, and slammed the thick door. Longarm heard the rasp of metal on metal as the Rurale dropped the peg back in the hasp.

Left in dark silence, Longarm fumbled in his vest pocket for the cigar he had refrained from lighting, fearing that any move he made might lead to an order from Calderon to empty his pockets. As he took out a match, he pressed his hand against the stubby little derringer that snuggled unobtrusively in his lower vest pocket.

Striking the match with a flick of his iron-hard thumbnail, he held it high for a moment, saw a kerosene lamp on a small table across the room, and shielded the match flame while he lighted the lamp. Before he adjusted the wick to stop its smoking, he lighted the cheroot and dropped the match just before it began to burn his fingers. Puffing on the cigar, he passed his eyes slowly over the room.

It was obvious that he was not the first prisoner to have been confined in the low-ceilinged chamber. Its furnishings were scanty: a bed with a bench beside it, the lamp table, and a wooden bucket under the table. The floor was not carpeted, but showed signs of much use, and the solid thud of his boot heels as he walked across the room told him its boards were three or four inches thick.

Two windows, both shut, cut the outer wall of quarried stone. Longarm stepped over to the nearest window and examined it. Through the glass he saw heavy board shutters. He tried raising the window sash, and the bottom pane lifted easily. When he unlatched the shutters and pushed them, the stout boards moved only a few inches before stopping with a thud. In the gap at their center he could see a gridwork of heavy iron bars fixed on the outer wall. Not only did the bars limit the shutters to a four-inch-wide slit when they were open, but they were too close together to allow even a very small child to slip between them.

Well, old son, that takes care of the windows, he told himself silently. *And there ain't no use banging on them walls, or on the door, either. They're so thick a man could*

61

pound on 'em with a ten-pound sledge and not bother no-
body outside. But that don't mean you're beat. There's a
lot more ways than one to skin a cat, and you ain't even
tried the first one yet.

With a shrug, Longarm turned to the other walls. When
he tapped the wall beside the door leading to the hall his
knuckles brought a solid thunk that told him it was made of
inch-thick boards. A tap on the abutting wall gave out the
same dull thud.

Sitting down on the side of the bed, Longarm puffed his
cigar thoughtfully. His eyes moved from wall to wall, door
to windows. No matter how long he studied his prison, he
saw no way that he could escape from it without tools that
he did not have.

At last he decided that all his thinking had gotten him
exactly nowhere. The room seemed uncomfortably warm
now, and he started to undress. Hanging his coat over the
chair, he glanced at the pillowless bed and folded his vest,
then placed it at the head, more to have the derringer close
at hand than because he felt in need of a pillow.

Levering out of his boots, he dropped them to the floor,
stepped out of his covert-cloth trousers, and tossed them
over his coat. Then he slid off his shirt and hung it over the
chair as well. After taking a final puff on the butt of his
cigar, he dropped it in the waste bucket, blew out the lamp,
and groped his way to the bed in the dark.

When the faint noise of metal grating on metal roused him,
Longarm woke, instantly alert. Instinctively, he started to
get up, then changed his mind. Lying back on the pillow,
but with one hand under his head closed around the derringer's grip, he closed his eyes as though he was still
asleep. The still air of the room moved in a gentle draft as
the door opened. There was a smack of flesh on flesh, a
smothered gasp, and then the door slammed shut.

Longarm lay quietly, aware that someone had been
thrown into his prison with him, but unable to see who it

was. The room was so quiet that he could hear the breathing of his fellow prisoner, but the new arrival neither moved nor spoke. A minute passed, then another, then Longarm decided to break the deadlock.

Keeping his voice low and his tone carefully neutral, he said, "I don't know who you are or what you're doing locked up in here with me, but ain't it about time we got acquainted?"

A gasp, the sound of a breath indrawn with surprise, came from the door. Silence took the room again for a full minute before Longarm's question got an answer. To his surprise, it was a woman who spoke.

"Por favor, no me daño!"

"Now, why'd I want to hurt you?" he asked.

"No conozco, pero el General—"

"Hold on," Longarm broke in. "Can you talk English?"

"Yes." Her voice was wavering and uncertain. It had lost its note of pleading, but was far from being firm. "I was not sure that you—"

Longarm interrupted her. "Hold up a minute. Maybe I better light the lamp, so we can both see who we're talking to."

"Yes," the invisible woman repeated, her voice a bit steadier now.

Longarm took a match and a cigar from his vest pockets and put the derringer in the palm of one hand. He closed his eyes and struck the match, its flame glowing redly through his eyelids. He waited the moment required for his pupils to lose their over-expansion after a period of darkness, then opened them. The woman was standing pressed against the door.

A swift glance was enough to tell him that she held no weapons. Both her hands were pressed to her face and her eyes were squeezed tightly shut. Longarm glanced at her while he stepped briskly to the table and lighted first the lamp, then his cigar. After the tip of the long, slim cylinder was glowing, he tossed the match aside and looked more carefully at his unexpected visitor.

From the configuration of her body, the woman was young. She kept her hands over her face, though he could see her fingers part and knew that she was looking at him. Only then did Longarm remember that he was standing there in his underwear.

"You ain't got a thing to be afraid of, unless Calderon sent you up here to worm information out of me," he said. "If that's why you're here, I'll tell you in advance that there's been women try to make me tell 'em things before, and I guess I know most of the tricks you'd use."

"No, no!" the woman exclaimed. "I am not trying to trick you!' She let her hands fall and Longarm had his first clear look at her face. To his surprise, she was young—little more than a girl. She went on, "You are his prisoner and so am I! I would not lift one finger to help him! If I could, I would kill him!"

Chapter 7

Longarm recovered quickly from the amazement that had swept through him. He said, "Being as it looks like we're in the same fix, maybe we better get our heads together. You might start out by telling me who you are."

"My name is Randita," the girl replied. "And I know about you from what I have overheard Don Claudio saying to his men."

"A first name don't give me much to go by," Longarm told her. He was studying her while they talked.

Randita could not have been more than twenty. She was in the full flower of youthful beauty. From her oval face, dark eyes rimmed with long lashes stared at him. Her eyebrows were full, accenting the ivory of her skin. Her cheekbones were high and flushed with excitement.

She had a small upturned nose above full red lips and a round firm chin. Her jet-black hair was pulled back from her oval forehead, caught up with a ribbon at the nape of her neck, and allowed to cascade down her back. The loose dress, a creamy silk, concealed her figure, but even its billowing fit could not conceal the high rise of her full breasts.

"Ain't you got some kind of family name?" Longarm went on when Randita did not respond to his suggestion.

"Please!" she said. "Do not ask me to tell you now. What Don Claudio has done to me shames my family's name."

"That ain't exactly your fault," Longarm pointed out.

"Even so, I feel to blame. You understand, he took me from his men after they had raided our *rancho,* and has kept me here for himself. And since then—"

"Wait a minute," Longarm broke in. "If you're Calderon's girl, why'd he lock you up in here with me? Did you make him mad or something?"

Randita was silent for such a long time that he thought she did not intend to answer. At last she sighed and asked, "You will not hurt me if I tell you?"

"Now, why would I do something like that? You ain't done nothing to make me lay a hand on you."

"I am supposed to, though."

"Now, that just plain don't make sense," Longarm frowned. Then he began to understand the devious scheme the fat man must have designed. "Mind telling me why you're supposed to get me all roiled up?"

After another long silence, she said reluctantly, "Don Claudio has sent me to kill you."

Without showing any surprise or raising his voice, he said, "I sorta had a hunch that's what you was going to say. Did he give you a gun?"

Randita shook her head. "No. But he gave me this." She slipped a hand into the neck of her low-cut dress and took out a long, wicked-looking sheathed stiletto. "He has told me to—"

"Get me into bed with you," Longarm suggested, when she searched for words.

She nodded. "Yes. But those are not the words Don Claudio used."

"What did he say he'd give you for killing me?"

"He promised me nothing," she replied bitterly. "I learned very quickly that Don Claudio does not reward those who carry out his orders. He punishes the ones who do not obey him."

She stopped abruptly, and Longarm could see indecision in her face. He waited patiently for her to continue.

At last she said, "Very cruel punishment."

Her teeth clenched, Randita pulled the neck of her loose-fitting dress over one shoulder and shrugged her arm free. A line of ugly red burns ran down her upper arm from the shoulder to the elbow.

"This he did to me when I refused to—" She stopped abruptly and turned her face away.

"To go to bed with him?" Longarm asked.

Nodding silently, her face still averted, Randita pulled the dress back over her shoulder. Her voice little above a whisper, she said, "I could not stand the pain, even if I found him as repulsive as a rattlesnake. And he has habits even more repulsive! He cannot be a man with a woman until—" She stopped abruptly, her face still averted.

Longarm waited for her to continue, but when she remained silent he took her attention away from the topic that was so obviously painful by asking, "How long have you been here?"

"Three, four months. I have lost track of time."

"Has Calderon been keeping you locked up?"

Randita looked up at him again. She shook her head. "But I have been watched."

"I guess you've told me all I need to know for right now," Longarm nodded. "You said you knew about me from what Calderon told his men. Maybe you better tell me what he said."

"Somewhere there is a prisoner of the Rurales who knows where much gold is hidden." Randita frowned. "Only the Rurales are not sure he is the one they believe him to be, and they have had you sent here to identify him. But Don Claudio wishes to get the gold for himself, and he made a plan to capture you before you reach the Rurales who have this man."

"Hold on," Longarm said. "This prisoner, you know what his name is?"

"I do not know his name. All I have heard him called is *El Anguila del Desierto.*"

"That's him," Longarm nodded. "The Desert Eel.

Where have the Rurales got him?"

"I cannot be sure, but I have heard Don Claudio speak of a place near Coyame. Where that is, I do not know."

"Neither do I, but I guess I can find out. Soon as I get outa this room, I mean."

Randita's jaw dropped as she stared at Longarm in amazement, then found her voice to ask, "You know of a way to escape from Don Claudio?"

"Well, I can't say I know how to get away quite yet, but there's bound to be some way or other," Longarm told her.

"*Señor* Long," she pleaded, "Will you take me with you when you go?"

"Oh, I had that in mind all along," he nodded. "And I don't aim to waste much time, because wherever that place called Coyame is, there's a bunch of real Rurales waiting to stand the Desert Eel up against a wall in front of a firing squad."

"And you wish to save him? You are his friend?"

"Let's just say I better be there before them Rurales gets to him," Longarm replied. For a moment he debated expanding his explanation, but the sudden guttering of the lamp drew his attention to it. He looked at the oil resevoir and saw that only a few drops of fuel were left. He went on, "Look here, Randita, we better do the rest of our talking in the dark. You don't mind that, do you?"

"I am not afraid of the dark, with you, *Señor* Long. And if we sit closer together, we can talk in whispers."

"Good," Longarm nodded. "You set still, I'll come over and set down by you. And if it's all the same to you, I got a sorta nickname that I answer to easier than I do all this *señor* business. It's Longarm."

"Then that is how I will call you."

Longarm blew out the lamp and puffed his cigar until its tip glowed brightly. Widened in the dark, Randita's eyes picked up the glow of the cigar. He fixed his mind on their location and dropped the butt of his cigar into the waste bucket, depending on his memory to guide him to the bed.

When he sat down beside her, Randita involuntarily drew away from him.

"Now, don't get scared," Longarm said, his voice gentle. "I ain't going to bother you none."

"I have no fear of you, Longarm," she replied, stumbling a bit over her first use of his nickname. "But Don Claudio—"

"Never mind about him. Now, I ain't seen this place by daylight, and I ain't got a notion how many men Calderon's got hanging around. Tell me about the men first."

"There is only one I am sure is always here," Randita said. "He is named Benito, the *mayordomo,* an old man, much older even than Don Claudio. Then there are some *peons* who come in by day, to cook and clean."

"How many."

"Sometimes three or four."

"They'd all be women, I guess?"

"Sometimes there is a man, to do small repairs."

"You got any idea how big a place this is?" When Randita said no, he asked, "What about the ranch hands? How many of 'em live in them shanties back of the house, here?"

"That I do not know. But the *vaqueros* never come to the house. I am sure Don Claudio does as my father did, gives all his orders for them to the chief *vaquero.* Even he does not come here every day, though."

"What about the people that visit him? A while ago you said something about a man called the general."

"That was Don Claudio I meant. It pleases him to be called 'General.' There are others who have been here a few times since I was brought here. I cannot tell you of them, though. When they arrived, Don Claudio locked me away at once."

"And Gomez, the Rurale that tricked me here?" Longarm asked.

"Of him I cannot be sure," Randita replied. "He has come here only two, or maybe three times since Don Clau-

69

dio made me his prisoner. That is all I can say."

"Well, it's better'n I hoped for," Longarm frowned. "By now, I'd guess you know your way around the place pretty good?"

"I know only the house. Outside I have been nowhere. It was dark when Don Claudio brought me here, and I was terribly afraid of him. I do not think——"

"That ain't so important," Longarm interrupted. "Because there ain't much of a way I can make a plan. All I can do is what seems best when the time comes."

"But how will you know when it's time?" Randita asked.

"I already know. It'll be the first time that door opens up. But you leave me to worry about that. I'll tell you what needs to be done, and all you got to do is what I say."

"I will do my best, Longarm," Randita promised. "And to know that you will take care of me has already made me feel better. Would you mind if I sleep now, while we are waiting?"

"That's about the best thing you can do. If you don't mind me stretching out on the other side of the bed, I'll just catch a few winks myself. I ain't had too much shuteye for the past day or so."

"I have no fear of you, Longarm," Randita told him. "Do as you wish. Maybe I will even sleep better, knowing you are so close to me."

Randita lifted her feet up on the bed and Longarm walked around to the other side. He slid his derringer into the folds of his vest and lay down. He lay awake for quite some time, but Randita had apparently fallen asleep as soon as she lay down, for her gentle regular breathing was the only noise that broke the silence of the chamber. After a while, Longarm slept, too.

Accustomed to sleeping with one ear open when he was in a place where danger threatened, Longarm snapped instantly alert when the soft scuffing of feet in the corridor outside reached his ears. He sat up, and beside him he heard Randita stirring.

The room was not as dark as it had been when he lay down, for through the gap between the window's shutters the sky showed in a pre-dawn grey.

He turned to Randita and said, "Quick! Get over there to the wall and stand where you'll be behind the door when it opens!"

Randita hesitated for only a moment before getting off the bed and moving to the wall. The footsteps outside could no longer be heard. Longarm slid his hand into the folds of his vest and found his derringer. Palming it, he padded to the foot of the bed and stood waiting. He heard the metallic click of the hasp that secured the door. Then it swung slowly open and the yellow light of a night lantern swept fanlike across the chamber. To Longarm's darkness-adjusted eyes, the lantern's glow was blindingly bright and he blinked to clear his vision. The man holding the lantern was little more than a dark blur to him.

Gomez's familiar voice broke the silence. "The girl!" he snapped. "Where have you hide her?"

Longarm's eyes were becoming accustomed to the brightness now. He could see Gomez in sharper outline. The Rurale was holding the lantern high with his left hand, a revolver in his right, his head swiveling from side to side as he looked around the room for Randita.

"Why, I ain't hid her, Gomez," Longarm protested. "She was here when I dropped off to sleep. Unless she got outa the window—"

Instinctively, Gomez switched his eyes to the window and its half-opened shutters. Longarm let the derringer slide forward in his palm. His forefinger curled around the trigger, but before he could raise the stubby little gun he saw a flicker of motion behind the Rurale. Then the bright steel of the dagger in Randita's hand flashed in the lantern light as she stepped silently up to Gomez and plunged the weapon into his back.

71

"Aie!" Gomez gasped, his gurgling cry trailing off to silence as he crumpled to the floor. The lantern fell, as did the revolver.

Longarm stepped forward quickly and picked up the lantern, but the kerosene that flowed from its reservoir had been ignited before the wick was snuffed out. The dark pool of coal oil was beginning to flicker, forming a stream of flame that ran across the wooden floor.

Randita was standing behind the dead Rurale's body, staring at the sprawled form of the man she'd just killed. She looked up at Longarm, her face twisted in shock.

"I—I did not intend to kill him—" she began.

"Never mind!" Longarm snapped. "If you hadn't, I would've got him. We got to move fast!"

He saw that his words were not getting through to Randita. Her mind was still blanked out from the shock of her action.

By now the flames of the burning kerosene were beginning to branch out and eat into the wooden floor as they spread. Longarm took two long strides to the bed. He grabbed his vest, stepped to the table, swept up his boots and the rest of his clothing, and tucked them under one arm.

As he started back to Randita's side, he glanced at Gomez, who lay facedown on the floor, and saw his own Colt still sticking in the dead Rurale's belt. Pausing only long enough to retrieve the revolver, he took Randita's arm and led her out of the room. At the door, he stopped and looked back.

One branch of the flames had crawled across to the bed now. The mattress and bedclothing were smouldering and beginning to char. Another trickle of fire was almost to the window, and a third was licking at the table legs. Longarm closed the door quickly, and the wide corridor was suddenly darkened, illuminated only by a hairline of red light that flickered through the crack between the door and the floor.

72

Moving into the hall had broken the spell of shock which had held Randita in its grip. There was comprehension in her eyes now as she turned to Longarm and asked, "What are we going to do?"

"We ain't going to do a thing but get outa here fast as we can," Longarm snapped. "You're all dressed, and it'll only take me a minute to get ready to move."

While he spoke, Longarm was shrugging into his shirt. He'd let his clothing fall in a heap on the floor. Now in the dim light he quickly pawed through the pile, pulled up his trousers, and jammed his feet into his boots. Buckling on his gunbelt, Longarm slid his Colt back into its holster, slipped on his vest and coat, and crammed his hat on.

Even in the few moments he'd spent dressing, the line of light below the door had changed its color. It was no longer red, but yellow, and heat from the burning room could now be felt through the door.

"You got anything in this place that you can't do without?" he asked Randita.

She shook her head. "Only a dress and some underwear that Don Claudio gave me. But I do not want anything that will remind me of him!"

"Where's Calderon's bedroom?" he asked.

"On the floor below."

"It'll take a few minutes for the fire to eat through the floor of that room," Longarm said. "But soon as the flames bust outa the windows, some of them *peons* in them shacks past the barns are going to see it. Which means we ain't got no time to spare."

Even as Longarm spoke, a finger of flame spurted through the crack below the door. It did not last, but almost at once another narrow tongue curled along the floor, then another. The corridor was suddenly filled with yellow light and a veil of smoke began to hang in the air, growing thicker each second.

"Look!" Randita cried as the fingers of flame merged into one sheet. "We must go now, Longarm!"

73

"We're leaving," he said, taking her arm and heading for the stairway. As they started down, groping their way in the flickering light that was beginning to trickle from the hall down the stairwell, he told Randita, "I want you to show me where Calderon's room is. Then you get on outside. Go through the front door and wait for me. I ain't going to waste no time, but there's some questions I got to ask Calderon before we go."

"Don Claudio's chamber is the third from the stairs. It will be on your left," Randita said. "But, Longarm—"

"Don't stop to argue!" he told her. "Just go on down and outside. I'll be there in a minute."

Longarm watched as Randita started down the stairs to the first floor, then turned and walked quickly along the wide corridor. Before he'd reached the third door ominous crackling noises were sounding from the ceiling as the flames swept through the dry, ancient wood of the floor above.

He was still several steps from the door he was seeking when it opened and Calderon came out. He was wearing a long nightshirt, its folds ballooning out over his immensely fat body as he moved. When he saw Longarm coming toward him, the fat man's face twisted in rage. He brought up a rifle that had been hidden by his voluminous nightgown.

Longarm had started to draw the instant he'd glimpsed the dark steel of the rifle's barrel. Before Calderon could level his weapon, the slug from the Colt tore into the fat man's chest and found his heart. His dying reflex tightened his finger on the rifle's trigger, but its slug thunked into the floor. Then the rifle clattered as it fell from his collapsing body.

For a moment, Longarm stood looking at the corpse, regretting that he'd never get the answers to his questions. Then he turned away and hurried down the stairs to join Randita.

74

Chapter 8

By the time Longarm got outside, shouts were coming from the huts that lined the lane beyond the house. Randita had not closed the massive door. She was standing a few steps away, peering around the corner of the *hacienda's* front wall. The wall itself was in shadows, but just beyond it the ground was swathed with flickering light. Longarm joined her and she turned to look at him briefly, then gestured toward the flame-dappled area that stretched from the side of the house.

"They're running up here," she said. "The *peons*."

Longarm peered around the corner of the building. Wide tongues of flame were shooting from the third-floor windows and shorter, thicker gouts of red were beginning to burst from the windows of the second floor. The fire had not yet reached the first floor. Its windows were still dark, but the flames from above lighted the building wall as well as the ground stretching away from in the direction of the barns and the *peons'* quarters.

Beyond the burning building, a straggling group of men and women were running toward the burning house. Some of them were only half-dressed, others were struggling into shirts or jackets. A few carried brooms or shovels, and some were swinging buckets as they ran. All of them were yelling and gesticulating.

"I don't see no sign of a well or a creek," Longarm said. "I'd guess there's a spring or something close by, but that fire's got such a start that they ain't going to be able to put it out, regardless of what they try."

"What are we to do when they get here?" Randita asked.

"We'll be gone by then," Longarm replied. "I don't imagine any of them is even thinking about us, or paying attention to anything but the fire. Come on. Let's move before they get too close. If we keep the building between us and them we'll likely get to the corral without them spotting us."

Turning, he led Randita along the front wall and onto the ground beyond. On this side of the house, the flames had not yet broken through the windows or roof, and the area they saw now was still dark. Instead of making a beeline for the corrals, Longarm led them in a wide arc that kept them well away from the approaching *peons*. By the time they started circling back, heading directly for the corrals now, the flames had run through the mansion's hall and inner walls and were reddening the windows on the dark side.

As soon as they had covered enough ground to get them well away from the *peons*, Longarm changed their course. Watching the activity around the mansion from the shadowed area through which they now moved, they hurried along in an arc that would get them to the corrals and stables.

By the time Longarm and Randita emerged into an area that was just beginning to be brightened by the sweep of the flames, almost all the *peons* had reached the *hacienda*. They were milling around the burning mansion, forced by the heat to keep their distance from it, their excited shouts rising above the roar of the flames, which were not beginning to spurt out of the dark side's windows.

Longarm and Randita reached the corral without attracting notice. Longarm halted and glanced at the ten or fifteen horses milling around inside.

"I ain't even thought to ask you if you can handle a

horse," he said. "Reckon I just taken it for granted."

"Don't worry, Longarm. I grew up on my father's *rancho*. I learned to ride almost as soon as I learned to walk."

Longarm nodded. "Well, go on and pick out a couple of horses. Don't waste too much time looking, but if you happen to see one with a U.S. Cavalry brand on it, I'd like to have it, if it ain't too much trouble to catch."

Randita nodded and started for the pole gate that closed the corral. Longarm ran on to the barn, only a few yards away. He glanced at the burning house as he moved. The entire structure was now enveloped in flames, and the *peons* were moving away from the intense heat, staring at the spectacle of the blazing building, their attention totally riveted on it.

Even inside the barn, the flames shed enough light for Longarm to see plainly. The first thing that caught his eyes was his own saddle gear, still entirely intact, his rifle and saddlebags apparently untouched, resting on a rack which held another dozen or so saddles. He gave the equipment a quick glance to make sure it was complete, then moved along the rack looking for a sidesaddle. He found none, and finally took the saddle and bridle that was next to his own.

By the time Randita came in leading a pair of horses, he had the saddles ready to throw on the mounts. She stood on one side to help get the job done faster, giving him a hand with the blankets and saddle pads, swinging the *cinchas* under the animals' bellies for him to draw tight and fasten.

With both of them working, saddling the two mounts was a ten-minute job. When he straightened up from buckling the last strap, Longarm stepped back and looked at Randita across the back of the second horse.

"Looks like we're ready to ride," he announced. "Now, just stick close to me. I aim for us to cut away from the house soon as we get past the end of the corral. Then we'll make a beeline for the road. I doubt there'll be anybody take after us."

"But what if Don Claudio should—"

"Calderon's dead," Longarm told her. "And his hands ain't going to have time to saddle up and take after us till we got so much of a lead they'd never catch up."

Randita's eyebrows had lifted in surprise when Longarm told her of Calderon's death, but she said nothing. She swung into the saddle of the pinto she had selected while Longarm mounted the cavalry horse. They rode out of the barn into the fire-bright night, saw that the house was still burning fiercely, great clouds of sparks being borne up now, riding the heated air far above the flames.

At some time while Longarm and Randita were busy in the barn, the *peons* had given up trying to put out the fire. They had huddled in a compact group out of range of the heat and were staring at the building or talking to one another. Their interest was so concentrated on the spectacle that they did not see the riders leave the corner of the corral and start toward the road.

Longarm and Randita looked back once or twice, but their main interest was in crossing the darkened countryside ahead. They rode up the gentle slope of the dimple in which the burning mansion stood, halted for a moment to gaze at the now-distant blaze, then toed their mounts back onto the path that would take them to the main road.

"You done a real good job back there," Longarm told Randita as they started down the slope. "I ain't much good at saying thank you, but you sure done what was needed when the chips was down."

"I only did what you told me to," she replied.

"Maybe so. But the main thing is, we got away with whole skins. Anyhow, we're free and clear, except I lost a day on doing the job my chief sent me down here to take care of."

They rode on in silence through the hushed pre-sunrise dawn that was ushering in the day. They got to the main road, and Longarm reined into it. Randita followed him, and they started picking up their pace again.

After they had covered a short distance, Randita turned to Longarm and asked, "Where are we going now?"

"All I can figure to do is go back to Ojinaga. For one thing, it's the closest place I know about. But that ain't the only reason. If I'm real lucky, there might be a trail there I can pick up. Anyhow, there's sure to be somebody there that can tell us where that Coyame place is located."

"I suppose it's as good a place as any," she agreed.

"We still got maybe an hour or so till it's full daylight," Longarm went on. "From what I seen of Ojinaga, it ain't such a much of a place, but there's bound to a hotel of some kind where you can stay."

"Stay?" Randita asked. "But I thought you would take me with you!"

"Now, going into the kind of place where the Rurales are holding prisoners ain't no kind of job for a girl like you, Randita," Longarm said. "The best thing you can do is send your folks word where you are, and have them come get you."

"I can't go home, Longarm!" Randita exclaimed. "You do not know my parents! I have disgraced my family's good name!"

"That's not any way to feel," Longarm protested. "It sure wasn't your fault that Calderon's outlaw bunch grabbed you."

"That would not matter to them. What has happened to me has ended any hope of the kind of marriage they expected to make for me. No, I cannot go home! Never!"

"You're upset and excited," Longarm said. "After a while you'll see things different."

"You do not understand my people," Randita replied. "But I do. No, Longarm. I cannot go home."

"Maybe you'll feel different after you've thought about it. You turn things over in your mind for a while, and let's see how you feel after we get to Ojinaga."

• • •

They came within sight of Ojinaga just as the rim of the sun broke the horizon. Longarm slowed their pace, and as they inched ahead he examined each house they passed. All of them looked alike, small two- and three-room adobe dwellings. None of the occupants were stirring yet. They passed two or three houses, all of them set far back from the road. Then he saw the one he was sure Gomez had taken him to, and reined in.

"You wait for me here," he told Randita as he swung out of his saddle. "This ought not to take long."

Approaching the squat adobe structure cautiously, Longarm rapped at the door. There was no sound from the house, and he knocked a second time, more insistently. When he still received no response, he tried a third time, and his repeated hammering finally brought a response.

"*Estoy cerrada! Volvere mas tarde!*" a woman's voice called through the door.

"Open up, lady! I got to talk to you!" Longarm responded.

"*De cual?*"

"*La noche ayer—*" Longarm began, and stopped while he struggled to find words from his limited Spanish vocabulary. Then it came to him suddenly that he could struggle for an hour with his smattering of Spanish, trying to understand and make himself understood, when Randita was only a few feet distant. Stepping away from the house, he called her. "Randita! I need some help here, because I don't speak Spanish too good. Would you come give me a hand?"

Randita slipped off her horse and hurried to his side. "What are you trying to find out?" she asked.

"That Rurale who brought me out to Calderon's place last night played a trick on me at this house here. I got to find out a few things from the woman inside there, but she don't speak English and I don't savvy your lingo good enough. Will you tell her I don't aim to hurt her, and all I want is for her to answer a couple of questions?"

"Of course I will," Randita nodded. She turned to the door and said loudly, *"No tienes miedo, señora! El señor solamente quiere hace unas preguntas!"*

"De cual?" the woman called.

"Acerca la noche pasada," Randita replied.

Slowly the door opened a crack. Longarm recognized the woman who peered out as the one who had served him the night before, and who had applied the fake bandage to Gomez's shoulder.

"Ask her where her husband is," Longarm said quickly.

"Donde esta su marido?" Randita relayed.

"No tengo marido. Soy viuda," the woman answered.

"She says she's a widow," Randita relayed.

"Ask her how about the fellow that was here last night."

"Era un hombre aqui a noche pasado. Que se llama el?" Randita asked.

"Su nombre no conozco. Era un amigo de Gomez."

"He was a friend of Gomez," Randita translated. "She says she doesn't know his name."

"If he wasn't her husband, he sure acted like he was." Longarm frowned. "Ask her again, Randita."

Her voice more insistent, Randita asked, *"Por favor, encite su memoria. Nesicitamos el nombre."*

"No conozco," the woman repeated. *"Sera un amigo de Gomez. Mira, niña! El Rurale Gomez hace un chiste! El me lo dijo que hace la chiste al Norteamericano. Es todo de cual!"*

"She said again that she doesn't know who the man was," Randita told Longarm. "She says he was a friend of Gomez, and they told her they were playing a joke on you."

"You think she's telling the truth?" Longarm asked.

"She doesn't seem to hesitate when she answers," Randita said. "I really don't think she knows."

"Well, since Gomez ain't going to give nobody no answers any more, I guess we hit a dead end," Longarm said

81

thoughtfully. "About all we can do is thank her and go on into Ojinaga. After that, it looks like the next stop's going to be Coyame, if I can find out where it is."

Ojinaga was still only half-awake as Longarm and Randita rode into the little town. The only activity they saw was on the wide dusty street near the town's center, halfway to the international bridge across the Rio Grande. There, a dozen or so men were gathered in front of a street vendor's cart, munching at tortillas and enchiladas.

Randita turned to him and said, "I guess if we expect to get anything to eat, it'll have to be here. I'm certainly ready for breakfast."

"I could use a bite myself," Longarm agreed. "We'll pull up and take time to eat."

When they approached the vendor's cart, the men who had been crowding around it scattered to give Longarm and Randita plenty of room. They stood a little aside as Longarm bought tortillas and tamales, and watched curiously as the two began eating. When their hunger had been partly satisfied, Longarm turned to Randita.

"This fellow oughta be able to tell us how to get to Coyame, if there is such a place," he suggested. "Maybe you better ask him about it."

Nodding, she turned to the vendor and asked, *"Por favor, adonde 'sta Coyame?"*

He indicated the international bridge with a sweeping gesture and replied, *"Al izquerida de la frente el punte. El camino segue al Rio Concho."*

"Gracias. Y tan lejos?" Randita went on.

Shrugging, he said, *"Trienta, tal vez curenta kilos."*

Turning to Longarm, Randita translated, "The road to Coyame starts on the left side of the bridge, and the town is twenty or thirty kilometers from here. That would be perhaps twenty or twenty-five miles. He said all we have to do is follow the course of the Concho River."

"That's the first I ever heard of a Concho River in Mexico," Longarm said. "But I guess he'd know. And if he's right about how far it is, we better get some grub from him to take along, because that's a real long day's ride."

"Then you are going to let me go with you?" she asked, her face brightening.

"Well, I can't just ride off and leave you here all by yourself," he replied. "Besides, I don't aim to stay at that Coyame place very long. All I got to do is identify that Desert Eel I told you about. Maybe on the way we can figure out what you're going to do when I go back to my regular job."

Longarm reined in and looked at the rugged country ahead. When Randita brought her horse to a stop beside him, he looked at her and shook his head.

In front of them the Rio Concho flowed, a thin trickling sheet of blue-green water that a horse could cross in two steps, in a bed half a mile wide. There was only the tan desert country on all sides, an occasional grey-green *ocotillo* plant breaking the monotony of the undulating earth. The sun had been in their faces for the past hour or more, and their eyes ached from squinting into its reddening rays.

"I don't know how far we've come from Ojinaga," he said, "but I'd guess maybe twenty miles by now. We sure ain't wasted no time. And from what I can see there still ain't a thing ahead of us but more rocks and sand."

"It will be dark soon," Randita said. "Will we go on, or stop for the night?"

"You sound like you're getting tired."

"A little bit. There was too much happening last night."

"Let's go on a little ways," Longarm proposed. "If we don't see that Rurale place pretty soon, we'll bunk down."

They moved on, the sun still in their eyes, but reddening now, a warning that it would soon be setting. When it had been reduced from a full shining circle to a half-circle that shed less and less light, Longarm began looking for a place to stop. He found one surprisingly soon, only a few yards from the river, a shelving rock jutting out from a sheer bluff to form a sheltered spot in the barren desert.

"This looks like as good a place as any," he said. "Lucky this is hot country, because all we got is saddle blankets. But we'll be up and on our way at first light tomorrow."

After tethering their horses and eating the rest of their tortillas while they sat on the saddle blankets below the little overhang, Randita looked at the shallow river and said, "I think I will bathe, Longarm. I am dirty from where I have been kept, much dirtier than the clean desert dust that has blown on us today."

"Go ahead," Longarm told her. "I'll just stretch out here and shut my eyes while you're bathing, so as you won't feel embarrassed."

He lay back on the blankets and closed his eyes. The strain of the past forty-eight hours and taken toll of even Longarm's superb physique. Though he'd intended only to rest, he dropped off to sleep.

A soft hand on his face aroused him, and when he looked up he saw Randita had knelt at his side. She had not put on her clothes after bathing, and when she bent forward to kiss him, her full breasts pressed on his chest. Instinctively, Longarm sought them with his hands, then shook his head as he moved his hands to cradle Randita's ribs and lifted her until her face was above his.

"If you figure you owe me something for giving you a hand back at Calderon's place, you're wrong," he said.

"I was not thinking of debts or payments," she replied. "I was thinking of you as a man. After Don Claudio's feeble caresses, I would like to feel a real man."

Randita bent forward, seeking Longarm's lips again, and this time he did not push her away. While they held their kiss, tongues entwining and lips clinging, he felt Randita's hands busy on his belt.

Longarm was more than ready. By the time Randita had

84

freed his shaft, the touches of her warm hands had brought him erect. Longarm took Randita in his arms and lifted her as he rose to his knees. As he lowered Randita to the blanket and sank into her, she sighed.

Chapter 9

Nodding toward the scattered cluster of adobe buildings he and Randita were approaching, Longarm said, "We oughta be in spitting distance of Coyame now, and the closer we get to that place, the more it looks to me like a pretty good bet for being Rurale headquarters. Don't it strike you the same way?"

"It certainly doesn't look like a ranch," she said. "There aren't any cattle in sight, and we haven't seen any all morning. And most ranches have a lot more barns and sheds and little houses for the *peons*."

"Well, it won't hurt to give it a try," he said. "If it ain't the headquarters, chances are the folks that live there will know where to find it."

Since shortly after daybreak, Longarm and Randita had been riding steadily with the sun at their backs. Their shadows were still long on the baked ground ahead of them, and the heat was just beginning to make itself felt. Their horses were beginning to act skittish after their long night's rest, their actions showing their hunger now, after having gone unfed since the previous day.

"Anyway, we're going to have to stop there," Longarm went on. "These nags have been good, but they got to be fed, and I don't mind telling you, my belly thinks my throat's been cut."

They turned off the road, heading for the buildings. While they were still only halfway to their objective, two men rode around the corner of the largest building and started toward them. Longarm turned to Randita.

"This is the place we're looking for, all right," he said.

"How can you tell?"

Longarm pointed to the approaching riders. "The hats and jackets they got on are a dead giveaway. Look at the way the sun's shining on all that gold thread embroidery. I never seen a Rurale yet that didn't sport as much gold thread as he could cram onto his hat and his duds."

By this time the two riders had reached hailing distance. One of them shouted, *"Hola! Alta ustedes!"*

"Shall we obey them, and stop?" Randita asked.

"I guess we better. No use rubbing 'em the wrong way. I've found out them fellows has got a habit of being just a little bit trigger-happy."

Longarm and Randita reined in and waited for the Rurales to reach them. Longarm took the opportunity to light a cigar from his diminishing supply while he studied the approaching men. His certainty that they were Rurales grew stronger. Both of them wore twin pistol-holsters on their belts, and at close range he could see that their boots as well as their *charro* jackets were heavily gold-embroidered. In his several encounters with the Rurales, both friendly and hostile, Longarm had learned that such decorations were almost always the mark of Mexico's elite national police force.

"Quien 'stan?" one of the Rurales asked as he and his companion reined in.

"My name's Long, Custis Long," Longarm said in the mildest tone he could muster. "I'm a deputy U. S. marshal, outa the Denver office, and this young lady's traveling with me. I got some business with you men, but that can wait. We run outa grub yesterday, and what we need right now's a bite of breakfast."

"You have sometheeng to prove who you say to be?"

Wordlessly, Longarm produced the well-worn wallet in which he carried his badge. He opened it and showed it to the Rurale, who looked questioningly at his companion. The second Rurale nodded and asked, "Your business is weeth who?"

"Captain Morales. I oughta been here yesterday, but one of your men give me a bum steer."

"What ees thees, bum steer?" the first Rurale asked.

Longarm did not explain, but countered with a question of his own. "You got a Rurale named Gomez here?"

"*Seguro*," the man nodded. "Why you are ask?"

"Maybe I better talk to Captain Morales before I answer any more questions," Longarm replied. "Now that you're satisfied who I am, suppose you take me and the lady to him."

For a moment the Rurales consulted with their eyes, then the man who'd been questioning Longarm said, "*Bueno*. You weel follow us, and we weel take you to the *capitan*."

Without a word being exchanged between the two Rurales, the one who'd been doing the talking wheeled his horse and started back toward the buildings while the second man gestured for Longarm and Randita to follow the first, then placed himself behind them. The little procession made its way to the largest of the buildings where Longarm and Randita followed the example of their escorts in tethering their mounts at the hitch-rail in front of the adobe structure.

Dismounting, the Rurales again bracketed Longarm and Randita as they went inside and entered a long hallway that extended the length of the building. The Rurale in the lead stopped at a door halfway down the hall, turned, and motioned for Longarm and the girl to enter.

Two men were in the room, sitting on opposite sides of a paper-strewn table. Both wore gold-embroidered jackets similar to those of the Rurales who had intercepted Longarm and Randita. The older of the men had a clipped grey mustache. His companion was clean-shaven, though the stubble on his swarthy cheeks had not felt a razor for two or three days. They looked up at the newcomers, but before either of them could speak, the Rurale who had taken the lead followed Longarm and Randita into the room.

"*Extranjeros, Americanos, quien quiere habla a usted, Capitan Morales,*" he said. "*El hombre dice que es mariscal Federal de los Estados Unidos. Tiene siñal correctamente.*"

"*Bueno, Sanchez,*" the officer nodded. "*Trata de nos. No es necessario quedarte.*" Addressing Longarm, but looking at Randita with a puzzled frown, the Rurale captain said, "I am Captain Morales. What is your business with me?"

"My name's Long, Captain," Longarm replied. "I don't talk your language very much, but I caught part of what your man told you. My chief's Billy Vail, in the Denver office. Billy sent me down here because he said you needed me to identify a prisoner you got, the one called the Desert Eel."

"Of course!" Morales exclaimed. "I received a telegram from Billy almost a week ago, but since then certain things have happened to keep me very busy." He turned to the second officer and said quickly, "I have not yet told you of this, Novalo. We will talk of it later, in private. Now, if you will excuse me, I would like to talk to the marshal and his companion."

"If I am to be in command here in a few hours—" Novalo began, but Morales cut him short.

"You will be fully informed," the older man said curtly. "Now, I'm sure there is other business you can attend to."

When Novalo left the room, Morales turned his eyes toward Randita and a frown slowly grew on his face. Without shifting his gaze, he said, "Forgive me for making such an observation, Marshal Long, but I did not expect you to bring a companion."

"Well, to tell you the truth, I didn't start out from Denver with this young lady. It's going to take a little time to tell you the whole story, but—"

Morales broke in. "Excuse me," he said. "I do not want to be discourteous."

Randita said to Morales, "When I saw you, I was afraid you'd recognize me, Tio Vici. Even if it has been a long, long time. And Longarm didn't ever mention that it was you he'd been sent here to meet, or I wouldn't be with him now."

Morales had been studying Randita while she talked. Now he said, "You have changed a great deal, my dear. Your father and mother, do they know you're here?"

"They are both dead," she replied. "Killed by bandits who raided and looted our *hacienda*. The devils captured me and kept me with them for a while, before the Rurales attacked their hideout and freed me. One of the Rurales took me then. He passed me on to Don Claudio—"

"Don Claudio? Claudio Calderon?" Morales broke in.

Randita nodded. "I was his prisoner until Longarm rescued me, just yesterday—or the day before."

"Calderon will pay for this!" Morales growled. "I will—"

Randita broke in, "He has already paid, Tio Vici. He is dead. His *hacienda* was burned to the ground when Longarm—"

Morales broke in again, turning to Longarm. He said, "I am curious about two things. First, what is this Longarm name that Randita calls you?"

"Oh, that's a sorta nickname I picked up. My friends call me that, and I got so I answer to it as good as I do my own real name."

"It is friendlier than his title, just as I call you Tio Vici, instead of Don Victorio," the girl said.

"I see," Morales nodded. "Then, if you should number me among your friends, Marshal Long—"

"Longarm, if you'd rather have it that way," Longarm said quickly. "But you said you was wondering about two things. What's the other one?"

"How did you come to find out about Calderon, Long-arm?"

"Why, the same way you did. From Randita."

"You understand, Tio Vici, Don Claudio talked freely after I—" She broke off, her eyes troubled.

"You do not need to explain to me, child," Morales said. "But what has happened to you is past. We will both forget it, for it changes nothing of my feeling for you." He turned back to Longarm. "Tell me now how you could escape from Calderon and bring Randita here."

"Well, that's pretty much of a yarn, too, Captain," Longarm replied. "Now, I ain't aiming to be pushy, but me and Randita ain't even had breakfast yet, and I don't talk so good when my belly's growling at me. Do you reckon we might go on talking while we get a bite to eat?"

"Of course!" Morales replied. "Come, we will go to my private quarters. I will have the cook send food there, and while you and Randita eat we can talk without being interrupted. Then we will be able to straighten out all the threads."

Settled into a combination bed-sitting room down the hall from the office, Morales said to Longarm, "There is another thing I have been wondering. How is it that you failed to meet the Rurale I sent to Ojinaga to bring you here?"

"Oh, I met him, all right. Except he turned out to be on the wrong side. I'm afraid you had a bad one in that Gomez fellow, Captain Morales."

"*Had* a bad one?" Morales frowned. "You sound as though—"

Longarm broke in, "He's dead."

Randita said quickly, "Longarm did not kill him, Tio Vici. I did. It was Gomez who brought Longarm to Calderon's *hacienda* instead of here, to you. Calderon ordered me to kill Longarm, and then sent Gomez to the room where we were both imprisoned. I killed him before—"

91

"Before he got to me," Longarm broke in. "So I brought her along to keep her away from Calderon's men."

Looking at Randita, Calderon exclaimed, "My poor child! What have these people done to you?"

"Now you see why at first I hoped you would not recognize me," Randita said. "It was Gomez who brought Longarm to Calderon's *hacienda,* Tio Vici. He was the outlaw's man, not yours."

Morales shook his head sadly. "My poor Mexico!" he sighed. "Our people have so much hope and so many trying to take the land from them! Even the Rurales have been infected by the greed!"

"This ain't the first time I've brushed up against some Rurales that's been playing both ends against the middle, Captain Morales," Longarm said. "But, thanks to Randita, I got here, and I'm ready to do that job Billy Vail said you wanted me to do. But maybe we better put that off for a little while and let you and her get things straightened out between you."

With many interruptions, Randita and Morales retied the threads of a long and very close friendship between her family and himself. As they talked in rapid-fire Spanish, Longarm ate and listened, catching a part of their conversation and being filled in by one or the other on what he'd missed.

When at last the pair had brought one another up to date, Morales said to Randita, "You know that I think of you as one of my own family, my dear. Now, I have some news for you. By the end of the day, I will have acquainted Captain Novalo of the affairs of this post. Tomorrow I leave for a new command in Jalisco. If you agree, you will come with me, and be the daughter that I never had."

Randita sat silent for a moment, then said, "Are you sure you will want me, Tio Vici? After what has happened—"

"What has happened is of no matter," Morales told her. "I will forget that, and so will you."

"Then I will go with you gladly," she replied. "But you

92

and I have been so busy talking that Longarm has not had a chance to tell you why he is here."

"I know of his main business," Morales said, "since I am the one who began it. But you are right, Randita. I should have talked to the marshal first." He turned to Longarm and went on, "This matter of *El Anguila del Desierto,* you are sure you can identify the man?"

"Oh, I don't have no doubt about that, Captain," Longarm replied. "I was with him for three or four days while I was taking him into Denver. That was after I'd arrested him for a post-office robbery in Arizona Territory. Of course, it's been a few years since I seen him last, but I'll know him, all right."

"Good," Morales nodded. "You have arrived here just in time, Long. I must question this Desert Eel before he stands before the firing squad tomorrow morning."

Longarm frowned and said, "You know, Morales, Billy Vail sent me all the way here from Denver just on your say-so. I still don't know why it's so all-fired important for you to be sure it's really the Desert Eel you got in your jail here."

"I am afraid I cannot satisfy your curiosity, Longarm. Will you take my word that it is truly important for the sake of my country that I talk with this man before he is executed?"

"Let me ask you something," Longarm frowned. "As far as I know, the Eel's just a plain, ordinary bandit, the kind that ain't worth one of your *pesos* to the dozen. If there's something going on here that Billy Vail didn't know about, he could get into a heap of trouble with the Justice Department because he sent me down here."

"I have a great regard for Billy," Morales said. "Do you think I would ask him to take the risk such a matter involves, unless it is important?"

"No, I don't reckon you would, except that Billy's back in Denver, and I'm here."

Again Morales sat silent for a moment. Then he nodded. "I can see your side of the question, Longarm. But I will ask you to be patient with me. There is still much that I must do before I leave."

"It don't look to me like an hour or two's going to make much difference," Longarm objected. "It ain't like you had to hurry to catch a train, or anything like—"

Morales broke in before Longarm could go on. "But that is exactly what I must do," he said. "I must catch a train that will get me to the federal capital without delay."

"Now, that don't make sense," Longarm frowned. "If there ain't no train that runs from here, how're you going to—"

Again Morales interrupted him. "Excuse me, Longarm. Now that I know you better, I see no reason to keep you in the dark. As you say, there is no railroad into Coyame now, but there is a new railway line being built from Ciudad Chihuahua to Ojinaga. Already it has reached within twenty kilometers of Coyame, and one day each week a passenger coach goes from the end of the rails to Ciudad Chihuahua, from where I can take the regular train to the capital."

"I take it the train you're looking to catch leaves from the railhead tonight or tomorrow, then?" Longarm asked.

"Tonight, and I must be on it without fail!" Morales said. "The fate of Mexico's future may rest on me catching that train!"

Longarm saw from the captain's agitation that the matter was truly important. He said slowly, "Well, I ain't going to ask you no questions about your own affairs, Captain Morales. Why don't you just wind up your business with Captain Novalo, and go on and catch your train? I'll put off talking to the Eel until tomorrow."

"You do not know Captain Novalo as I do, Longarm!" Morales exclaimed. Dropping his voice to a half-whisper, he went on, "He is younger than I am, but his mind is like those of the old Rurales, who lived by the law of the gun!"

"Shoot first and ask questions later," Longarm nodded.

"We got a few of that kind left up north of the Rio Grande, Captain."

"Novalo has another name among our men," Morales said. "He is also called *El Carnicero*."

"The Butcher?" Randita broke in. She had been listening to the discussion between Morales and Longarm without interrupting. With a glance at Longarm, she added, "Gomez was another of that kind. I cannot blame you for not trusting him, Tio Vici."

"Now, I didn't come down here to Mexico to get caught up in private fusses between your Rurales, Captain," Longarm said. "You come right down to it, I ain't really got no business here at all. Billy Vail's my chief, and he sent me here to do you a favor. Well, I'm here, and all I want to do is take a look at this Desert Eel and start back to Denver. So I'd be real obliged if we can take care of that little job and let me be on my way."

"I cannot blame you for feeling as you do, Longarm," Morales nodded. "And we will attend to your business without any more delay. But I cannot miss the train to the south! I have information which *el Presidente* Diaz must have at once."

"I wouldn't want you to miss that train on my account," Longarm said. "If your business in Mexico City's all that important, and you're pressed for time, you go on. It don't make no difference to me whether you or Novalo takes care of my job in coming here."

Morales looked at Longarm, his face drawn into a thoughtful frown, then said, "I see no reason why you should not know. You may even have guessed by now, it has to do with a plot to overthrow *el Presidente*."

"I had a pretty good hunch there was something important going on," Longarm nodded. "Well, I ain't going to waste a lot of time. All I need to do is get a look at this fellow you think is the Desert Eel, and I'll know for sure whether he is or not."

Morales sat silently for a moment, then shook his head.

"No," he said, as much to himself as to Longarm, "I cannot ask you to risk becoming involved in my affairs."

"It looks to me like I already am," Longarm said. "And if Billy Vail thinks enough of you to send me all this way to give you a hand, I oughta be ready to take on a little bit more'n I was supposed to. What is it you got in mind?"

"It is more than the loot of *El Anguila del Desierto* that I must recover," Morales said slowly. "He and some of his outlaw gang held up a bank in Toluca. Now, Toluca is a small place, and the bank was not a large one. But in one of the safety-deposit boxes they looted there were papers which must not be made public. If what they hold was known, it could bring on a revolution in Mexico and perhaps the downfall of *el Presidente* himself."

"So that's the way of it!" Longarm exclaimed. "I guess that could mean a whole lot of trouble for folks on both sides of the Rio Grande, my country the same as yours."

"It would, without doubt," Morales nodded.

"It ain't that I like your president all that much, Captain, but I don't reckon the President of the United States would cotton much to having all hell break loose in his back yard."

"I can assure you that *el Presidente* Diaz would feel the same way," Morales said soberly.

"You go about your business, then," Longarm told the captain. "I'll fix it up so I can talk private with the Desert Eel and find out where he's hid his loot. And, by some hook or crook, I'll do my best to get you back them papers."

Chapter 10

For a moment Longarm and Morales sat staring at one another across the table. Then the Rurale said, "If you will indeed do this, I can go on to Mexico City with a lighter heart."

"Now, if you knew me a little bit better you'd know I don't go back on my word," Longarm told the captain. "I guess you got a safe place where I can send you anything I find?"

"Of course. You can send it to—"

"Hold on, Captain Morales," Longarm interrupted. "Don't tell me something I might forget. Just write it down on a piece of paper, a little tiny piece I can slip in my wallet back of my badge. That way, there ain't nobody likely to find it and I ain't going to forget it."

"I can print it in very small letters, if you wish, Tio Vici," Randita volunteered. "I remember how big your writing is."

"Do so, then," Morales agreed.

He took paper, pen, and ink bottle from the drawer of the table and pushed them to Randita, then bent over her and whispered in her ear while she printed the address on a corner of the paper. Tearing off the corner, now covered with three lines of tiny printing, Randita folded it into a square no bigger than a postage stamp and handed it to Longarm. He slid his wallet from his coat pocket and tucked the paper behind the badge.

"I guess that settles everything," he said to Morales and the girl. "Now, you can just tell Novalo to take me into whatever kind of place you use for a jail here and I'll spin him a yarn about having to talk to the Desert Eel in private, and that'll be that."

"Suppose the Eel will not talk to you?" Morales frowned.

"Don't worry about that," Longarm said with a confidence he was far from feeling. "I'll figure out some kind of proposition Novalo will listen to, one that'll let me walk outa here with the Eel."

"I wish you luck," Morales said. He turned to Randita. "I do not suppose you brought anything away from the place where Calderon was keeping you prisoner?"

"I had nothing to bring. Only the clothes I was wearing," she told him.

"I am packed, ready to go as soon as I clear up a few last details with Novalo," Morales said. "I will go and find him now. As soon as I've given him a few final details, we can start for the railhead. I would not want to miss this train. There will not be another one going to Chihuahua for a week."

"I reckon I better go along when you meet Novalo," Longarm volunteered. "And make sure I'm going to get to talk to the Eel later on today."

Leaving Randita to wait in Morales's quarters, the two men made their way to the office. Novalo was sitting in the place Morales had occupied earlier.

"Are you ready at last to pass over your command?" he asked as Morales and Longarm came in. He indicated Longarm with a flick of his hand. "And what about him?"

"Marshal Long wants only to talk to one of the prisoners who is awaiting execution," Morales replied. "I am sure you will be able to oblige him. He is in no hurry. You and I will have all the time we need to take care of the few things left to be settled between us before I must go."

"If you'll tell me where your latrine is, I got a little bit of private business of my own that I need to tend to while you two men are talking," Longarm said.

"Turn right as you leave the front door," Morales said. "You will see it some fifty yards away, past the corner of the building."

Longarm started for the door. He went through the shadowed hall, and though his eyes were blinking when he went out into the moon-bright sunshine, he saw at once the building he was looking for. He was within a few steps of the latrine when a pair of brown-robed priests, the cowls of their robes drawn over their heads, appeared from behind it. One of them held up his hand in a signal for Longarm to stop.

"What's on your mind, Padre?" Longarm asked.

"Veremos a Capitan Morales," the robed man replied, his voice muffled by the thick fabric of his cowl.

Longarm pointed to the headquarters building. "He's in there. Go around in front and in the door. You'll find his office about halfway down the hall."

"Gracias, hijo mio," the priest replied. *"Santiguarde Dios."*

Longarm hurried on past the robed men and into the latrine. When he came out a few minutes later, he was surprised to see them standing at the side of the headquarters building, their heads together, their arms waving. From their attitudes it was clear to Longarm that they were not praying, but before he could decide what their odd behavior meant, their discussion ended. They started walking along the side of the headquarters building.

Just before they disappeared around the corner, Longarm saw both of the robed men drop their hands to their hips and swivel their wrists in a quarter-turn. The gesture meant only one thing to him. It was one he'd seen many times before, the move an experienced gunfighter makes to adjust his pistol holster in the moments before facing a shootout.

Longarm took off at a dead run toward the headquarters

building. He circled in the direction of the door, trying to catch sight of the pair before they entered the building, but the distance was too great. When the door came in sight the only glimpse he got of the robed men was a swaying fold in the skirt of one of their brown robes vanishing through the opening.

There was no way for Longarm to run faster than he was already going. He drew his Colt as he ran and reached the door of the headquarters building. Blinking his eyes as he entered the hall, dim to him after the bright sunshine, he saw the two robed men moving slowly down the hall. They were peering into each open door they passed, their hands busy pulling up the loose skirts of their habits. When the thunking of Longarm's boots sounded on the wooden floor they turned, their hands on the butts of the revolvers that had been concealed under the loose, flowing habits.

Longarm's Colt was already in his hands. His first shot dropped the man nearest him, but the second man was leveling his weapon by then. The surviving phony priest had his pistol up by the time Longarm triggered his Colt again and its heavy slug sent the man staggering backward. Its impact did not stop the action of his trigger finger, though. His dying reflex closed his finger and the weapon roared, its bullet thunking into the hall floor as he crumpled and fell.

Echoes of the shots were still reverberating in the hallway when Novalo came running from the office, Morales following close behind him. Novalo was drawing his revolver, and for a moment Longarm thought the Rurale was going to shoot, but he recognized Longarm in time to let his gun hand drop to his side. Then both he and Morales spoke at once in rapid-fire Spanish, their words tumbling out in such a confused chatter that Longarm could not understand what either of them said.

Outside, excited shouts were sounding as the Rurales who had heard the shooting rushed toward the headquarters building. By the time Novalo and Morales reached the bodies and stopped to examine them, the first of the other Rurales was at the door of the long corridor.

Novalo had dropped to one knee on the floor beside the sprawled forms of the foiled assassins and was pulling the cowl from the face of the one nearest him. Morales looked at Longarm, who still stood with his Colt in his hand.

"How did you recognize them as impostors?" he asked.

"I didn't till I seem 'em lining up their guns to draw," Longarm replied. "They stopped me outside and asked where they could find you. I just figured they was some sorta traveling priests looking for a meal, or maybe wanting to give you some kinda message."

By now Novalo had uncovered the face of the second disguised gunman. Looking up at Morales, he asked, *"Conoces ellos?"*

Morales glanced quickly at the bodies and shook his head. *"Son extranjeros, entrandos."*

Men from the outside were crowding into the hall now, cutting off the small amount of light that came through its only outer door. Novalo looked up and commanded, *"Buscales el campo, inmediatamente! Es posible hay mas escondidos ahi!"*

"Mires tambien a caballos," Morales added. *"O una carreta. Andales!"*

After the Rurales had scattered, leaving Longarm alone with Morales and Novalo, Longarm glanced down the corridor and saw Randita standing in front of the door of Morales's room. She was gazing at the sprawled bodies of the gunmen, her face drawn into a worried frown. He had no idea how long she'd been there, but he shook his head and motioned unobtrusively for her to go back into the room. She nodded and disappeared through the doorway.

Morales and Novalo were hunkered down beside the bodies, searching the pockets of the dead men and carrying on a low-voiced conversation. Their voices were too low for Longarm to make out what they were saying, even if his command of Spanish had been enough to allow him to understand their words. At last the two Rurales stood up.

"I think we owe you a great deal, Longarm," Morales said. "These men certainly intended to kill one or both of us."

"How did you happen to come to the door at just the right time?" Novalo frowned.

"It wasn't happenstance," Longarm replied. He explained quickly how the disguised killers had asked him for directions, how he'd seen them still standing outside the headquarters when he came out of the latrine, and concluded by saying, "When they started inside, I seen both of 'em reach back to feel how their pistol holsters was setting, and I knew right then they wasn't real *padres*. So I busted into a run and got here just in time."

"Fortunately for Captain Novalo and me," Morales nodded. "I don't suppose you saw which direction they came from?"

Longarm shook his head. "They could've come from anyplace."

Novalo frowned. "Morales and I are not unaccustomed to facing danger, Long, but we would most certainly be dead men if you had not been alert. Now, I must go and arrange for these bodies to be taken away and buried. I will discuss your business here when I return, Marshal Long." He turned to Morales. "You and the girl will be leaving soon?"

"As soon as possible," Morales nodded. "I have told you everything that is necessary, and if the sergeant carried out my instructions, my personal effects were loaded on the wagon while we were having our talk. I wish to leave as soon as possible. The road to the railhead is bad, and it will take the wagon a long time to get there."

With a curt nod, Novalo swiveled on his boot heel and walked down the hall to the door. Morales watched him go outside, then turned back to Longarm.

"I do not think you will have any further trouble with Novalo," he said. "He has agreed that you will be given time to question *El Anguila del Desierto* before the execution takes place tomorrow morning. I wish you success, *amigo.*"

"Well, your friend Novalo ain't the easiest man in the world to get along with," Longarm replied. "But I guess it'll all work out right. Now, I'll just walk along down the hall with you and say goodbye to Randita."

Because Morales was present, Longarm's parting with Randita was stiffly formal. She kept her eyes turned down until the last moment, but as she followed Morales down the hall, she turned for a moment and touched her fingertips to her lips, then blew across her palm in Longarm's direction. Before Longarm could wave in reply she vanished through the door.

Well, old son, Longarm mused as he started back up the long hallway to wait for Novalo's return, *it's time for you to start thinking again about getting on with the job you come here to do. Here it is, another day just about gone, and if you don't close up this case and get back to Denver right fast, Billy Vail's gonna he madder'n a wet hen.*

Reaching the door of what was now Novalo's office, Longarm settled down in the chair nearest the door. Fishing a cigar out of his vest pocket, he leaned back, propped his feet on the table, lighted the cheroot, and resigned himself to waiting. A calendar on the wall across the desk caught his eye and he looked at it for a moment, counting the days since he had left Denver and the days his return would require. After a moment he shook his head unhappily and resigned himself to wait.

Almost half the cigar had become smoke and ash before voices in the corridor warned him of the new commander's return.

Novalo was saying, *"Dijo otra vez que es impossible, padre! Se obligado tiran los prisoneros mañana!"*

Longarm jumped up as a priest entered. He wore a robe and the reversed collar of his calling, and on his chest was a crucifix hanging from a bead necklace. He turned at once to face Novalo, who had seen Longarm and stopped just inside the doorway.

"Nada es impossible!" the priest said. *"Y sera desgraciado los Rurales si llevate a cabar estos prisoneros mañana!"*

"Marshal Long!" Novalo exclaimed when he saw Longarm. For the first time his voice held a friendly inflection. "I was going to send a man to find you. This is Father Eusebio. He has come to give the last rites to the condemned prisoners." Turning to the priest, he went on, "This is the United States marshal of whom I spoke, the man who caught the intruders who were coming to assassinate me."

"Your arrival was timely," Father Eusebio commented as he took Longarm's hand with a firm grip. "I do not know that you are of the faith, but if you should wish absolution—"

"Well, I thank you, but I reckon I'll pass, Father," Longarm replied. "Not that it'd hurt me none, but all I am is a backslid Baptist."

"Father Eusebio is sure the men who tried to kill Morales and me were not priests," Novalo went on. "They had no tonsures and the clothes they wore under their robes were not such as a priest would have on. For my part, I believe they came here to free the prisoners who are to be executed."

Breaking into Novalo's remarks, the priest said, "And I was also telling the captain that to execute those prisoners tomorrow would be an insult to the Church. I'd be interested to know if you share my belief."

"Well, now," Longarm said slowly, "it ain't my job to get wound up in whatever argument you and the captain was having."

"Perhaps you'd like to leave," Novalo suggested. "Then Padre Eusebio and I will continue our debate in private."

"Maybe I better," Longarm agreed. "Seeing as how you ain't going to shoot them prisoners till tomorrow, I can look at 'em later on, when you got the time to spare." He was turning to leave when the priest spoke.

"A moment!" he said. "Captain Novalo tells me that you are a federal officer of the United States?"

"That's right," Longarm replied.

"And that you have an interest of some kind in the prisoners who are to be executed tomorrow?" the priest went on.

"Well, all the interest I got is in one of 'em," Longarm said. "I come here to look at him and see if it's a man we been hunting for up north of the border."

"One man or many, it makes no difference," the priest said quickly. "Do me the favor of staying for a moment and help me persuade Captain Novalo to postpone the execution."

"Not being disrespectful, but that ain't rightly none of my business," Longarm replied.

Novalo opened his mouth to say something, but the priest saw him start to speak and waved him to silence. "Let me explain, Marshal—Long, is it?" he said.

When Longarm nodded and started to reply, Novalo broke in. *"Padre—"* he began, but when the priest gestured for him to remain quiet he closed his mouth and stood frowning angrily.

Turning back to Longarm, the priest went on, "I do not argue that the prisoners deserve mercy, you understand. They have been convicted under our nation's laws. But tomorrow is one of the holiest days of our church calendar, Marshal Long. When I was asked to come here today and administer the last rites to those who were to die, it suddenly struck me as being almost a sacrilege to kill people on such an occasion."

Speaking quickly, Novalo managed to break in and say, "I have tried to explain to the *padre*, Long, that I have no choice but to carry out my orders. Please tell him what we both know, that this is a matter for the law, not for the Church!"

"Everything which is an injustice is a matter for the Church, my son!" the priest said angrily. "To kill is bad enough at any time, and we in holy orders feel sorrow even for the criminal who is executed. But to kill on such a day as tomorrow is an insult to the Church!"

"But my orders—" Novalo began, only to be waved to silence once more by the priest.

Before the priest could speak, Longarm took advantage of the break in the angry exchanges between Novalo and the cleric.

"Maybe I ain't got no business butting in on this," he said. "But it looks to me like both of you can have your way if you work it right."

Novalo and the priest both stared at him in astonishment. At last Novalo said, "That cannot be, Long. You are wrong, of course. Tomorrow is tomorrow. It cannot be changed."

"And on that, I agree with the captain," the priest said.

"Let's see if I'm wrong," Longarm suggested. "Now, *padre*, what's the date of your holy day?"

"Why, tomorrow, of course. Friday, the fifteenth day of the month."

"And what date's on the order you got for them executions, Novalo?" Longarm asked.

"You have already heard the *padre* tell you. It is the same, Friday, which is still the fifteenth of the month."

"So it is," Longarm agreed. "And you'll have to send in a report that the executions were carried out, I guess?"

"Of course. Is it not the same in your country?" Novalo said.

"Oh, sure. And from what I've seen, them reports gets tucked away someplace and nobody ever looks at 'em again, or if they do they don't look at 'em too careful." He paused a moment, then went on, "Now, if you'll take a look at that calendar on the wall, you'll see that tomorrow's Friday the fifteenth. But in the month right next to it, Saturday was the fifteenth."

106

"What does that signify?" Novalo asked after he'd studied the calendar for a moment.

"Be quiet, Captain!" the priest said. "I think I can see where Marshal Long is leading us." Turning to Longarm, he said with a smile playing at the corners of his mouth, "You must have been schooled by the Jesuits, my son."

"I never did have much schooling," Longarm replied, "but that don't mean I can't do a little figuring." He turned back to Novalo. "What I'm getting at, Captain, is that if you was to look at whatever execution order you got from your headquarters, all it'd have on it is figures, the month and the date. It wouldn't name the day, like Monday or Tuesday or Wednesday."

"That is true," Novalo agreed.

"Now, suppose when you set down to fill in that report you just happened to look at the wrong month on the calendar," Longarm continued, "and you filled in the report wrong. Would it get you into any kind of trouble?"

Novalo frowned thoughtfully and shook his head. "I do not see why, as long as I had ordered the executions and my men had obeyed my order."

"It would be a human mistake," the priest put in. "And, in any case, the order would have been carried out."

Looking from one to the other, Longarm asked, "Then why not do it that way?"

Both Novalo and the priest were silent for a moment as they studied the calendar. Then they looked at one another and both nodded with satisfaction.

"I would be greatly pleased, Captain Novalo, if you were to order the execution for the day after tomorrow," the priest said quickly.

His eyes returning to the calendar, Novalo said, "Such a little error would leave me blameless. I would have carried out my orders, and that is the important thing. Anyone can make a small mistake, such as reading the wrong month of a calendar."

Longarm said, "Not that it makes much never-mind, but

107

I'd feel better, too. Today's just about gone, and I still ain't had a chance to talk with that prisoner I come here to question."

"It will be done, then," Novalo nodded. "Will that make you feel better, *padre?*"

"Of course! I only ask that the holy day be unmarred by the executions. I do not argue anything more," Father Eusebio said.

"Bueno," Novalo exclaimed. "Now, I have a bottle of very old *aguardiente* in this drawer. Let us drink to the settlement of a dispute between the Church and the state!"

Chapter 11

When Longarm woke up the following morning, the pale light of pre-dawn that ushered in the sunrise was outlining the window of the small room he had been given in the headquarters building. As was always the case, he snapped into the new day fully awake the instant his eyes opened, and his first thought was that the small breeze that had been blowing fitfully when he went to sleep was already growing warmer with sunrise.

At his bedtime the room had been uncomfortably warm, unlike the cool nights to which he was accustomed in mile-high Denver. Longarm had turned and tossed for several minutes before swearing mildly at the climate south of the Rio Grande. Then he'd stripped off the longjohns he usually wore to bed and pushed the blanket away. Before he'd gone to sleep, the breeze coming through the window had cooled a bit, but the tiny flow of air that was now stirring in promised another hot day.

This'd be one hell of a place for a man to have to live in, old son, he told himself as he rolled on his side and fumbled for a cheroot and matches in the pockets of his vest, which hung on the back of a chair beside the bed. *Summer ain't here yet, and it's already getting hot. Even a little bit of snow might be better'n this place here.*

A flick of his thumbnail started the match blazing and a puff or two on the cheroot created a cloud of smoke which flowed toward the glassless window of the little room.

Lying back, Longarm puffed again and watched the roiling threads of smoke while he contemplated the job that awaited him later in the day.

Your case here's right close to being wound up, old son, his thoughts ran. *It ought not take two minutes to make sure that prisoner the Rurales has got is really the Desert Eel, and you can start back home. Let the Rurales make the Eel tell where he's hid his loot before they stand him up against a wall.*

A rattling of the doorknob broke into Longarm's thoughts. He reached for the Colt, hanging in its holster from the back of the chair beside the bed, and had the weapon in his hand and ready when the door opened and a woman peered around its edge.

"Just stop right there," Longarm said. Almost before he'd finished speaking he realized that the woman might not understand English, for in spite of his warning she'd come into the room and stopped at the foot of the bed.

"Ees all right," she said. "You do not need *pistola*. I only breeng you message."

"Who are you, anyway?" Longarm asked. "I ain't seen you around here before."

"I am Saffrona, *señor,*" she replied. "Ees my job to clean up rooms. But *ahorita, el capitan* Novalo ees send me weeth message for you."

As she spoke, the woman's eyes were studying Longarm's muscular frame, and belatedly he realized that he was lying totally naked under her engrossed scrutiny. He groped for the blanket and pulled it up to his waist, then took the cigar out of his mouth while his eyes flicked over his unexpected visitor.

Saffrona was younger than most of the *lavanderas* he'd seen around the Rurale headquarters. Her nose was aquiline, her lips full, her chin just a bit on the sharp side, and her eyes jet-black. Her age was impossible to guess. She could have been almost any age from twenty to thirty.

Actually, it was hard for Longarm to tell a great deal

110

about Saffrona. Her head was bound up in a scarf and, like the clothing of the other women he'd noticed, hers was loose and badly fitting. She had on a billowing blouse of lightweight cotton cloth over a chemise or some sort of heavier underblouse. Her skirt billowed from her hips and fell almost to her ankles. Her feet were bare, thrust into plaited leather *huaraches*.

"Well, if Novalo's sent you with some kind of message, maybe you better tell me what it is," Longarm suggested.

"El capitan would like for you to join him at breakfast in hees office," she said. "There ees no hurry, he say. *Media hora, mas or menos."*

"I hadn't even started thinking about being hungry yet," he smiled. "But if you're going back there right away you can tell the captain—"

Saffrona broke in to say, *"El capitan* say there ees no hurry." She shrugged, her eyes flickering over Longarm's bare torso. She dropped her voice and pulled her shoulders back, and with her movement the loose blouse suddenly outlined the twin globes of her breasts. "Eef you have something you weesh me to do, I can stay."

Longarm had no trouble understanding her meaning. He'd seen enough encampments of various kinds during his earlier visits to Mexico to know about the *lavanderas*. Called "laundresses" out of the innate courtesy of the Latins, they were among the vast army formed by laborers of the cities and huge estates which had been torn apart during the revolutions which had swept across Mexico for almost a half-century. Some were satisfied simply to serve as prostitutes, others had formed at least semi-permanent relationships with one of the soldiers.

There was no such thing as a permanent relationship for most of the *peons* who found themselves members of the fighting forces which competing military leaders gathered in search of power over the revolution-torn nation. When a *lavandera's* man fell in battle, she found another or another found her. Universally, the *lavanderas* who attached themselves to the army or the Rurales offered the men more highly personal services besides washing and mending their clothes and cooking their meals.

Longarm looked at Saffrona for a moment, then told her, "Now, I thank you for your offer, Saffrona, but if I'm going to have breakfast with the captain in half an hour or so, that wouldn't give us time to do more'n barely get started."

"You are right," she shrugged, then sighed and added, *"Que lastima! Otra vez,* another time, no?"

"Maybe," Longarm agreed. "I reckon you'll be around where I can find you?"

"Sí. And do not to worry, at thees time I have no man who ees theenk I am belong to heem alone."

"Well, that's good to know, too, I guess," Longarm said. "Now, you better run along. If I'm going to have breakfast with the captain, I got to hop outa bed and get ready."

He waited until Saffrona left the room, then got up and started dressing. He'd reached the stage of shoving his feet into his boots before the idea that he'd gotten from Saffrona's visit took its full shape.

Standing up, he strapped on his gunbelt and slid his arms into his vest, moving more slowly now as he thought. He looked at the inch or so of Tom Moore that remained in the bottle, and regretfully decided to forego any inspiration that his usual eye-opener might bring. Replacing the bottle in his saddlebag, Longarm walked down the deserted corridor to Novalo's office. The door was open, and when he looked inside he saw the Rurale captain waiting at his desk.

A large earthenware platter stood on the desk. A steaming coffeepot sat in the center of the platter and around its edges were the flat sugar-coated buns which in Mexico were called *biscochos*. Beside the platter, cups stood waiting. Abandoning his faint hope that the captain would have something a bit more filling than the universal breakfast of the country, such as eggs and bacon, Longarm sat down across from Novalo.

"It's right nice of you to ask me to have breakfast with you, Captain," he began. "I might've had a little trouble if I'd started out looking for grub on my own."

"That thought occurred to me," Novalo nodded. "Be seated, and help yourself to coffee and *biscochos*. We can talk as we are eating." After Longarm had settled into a chair and filled a cup, the Rurale went on, "it also struck me that you might wish to go early to question this man you have come here to see. I would not like to have your mission delayed, and the prisoners will be executed at daybreak tomorrow morning."

"I guess the *padre* was glad you and him made a deal?"

"He seemed satisfied," the Rurale shrugged. "But to me it was a foolish gesture that he made. One day is like another to us. We carry out orders without bothering to look and see what saint's day it might be. Now, tell me, do you think you will be able to persuade this *Anguila del Desierto* to give you the information you are after?"

His mouth full, Longarm nodded. After he had swallowed and had a sip of coffee, he said, "I might have to twist his arm a little bit, but that don't bother me. He ain't the first prisoner I've run into that's told me what I need to know."

"Good," Novalo nodded.

Longarm went on, "But I don't mind telling you, Captain, I'd a sight rather have a carrot to use on this Eel than a club."

For a moment the Rurale did not reply, then he asked, "You are suggesting that he be offered something in return for the information? But what? The man knows he will be shot tomorrow!"

"Why, maybe just making him happy tonight might be enough."

"Making him . . ." Novalo's puzzled frown suddenly vanished, and was replaced by a smile. "Ah! I understand!

113

A woman to share his bed on his last night? Is that what you are saying?"

"That'd be one thing," Longarm nodded. "Or maybe just let him take a walk out in the open air—with a guard along, of course. Only I wouldn't want to make him no promises unless it's all right with you."

Novalo sat silent for a moment. Then he said slowly, "It is not a custom of our country to give a condemned prisoner his last wish, as it is in yours. But I cannot see that any harm will be done by trying it. You have my permission to do as you see fit in making the man such an offer, Marshal Long."

"I noticed there's plenty of *lavanderas* around your place here," Longarm said. "I don't guess there'll be any trouble finding one of 'em that'd oblige?"

Shaking his head, Novalo replied, "In a permanent station such as this one, we have more than our share of *lavanderas*. Any of them will share the blankets of a man who offers her a meal or a drink, or sometimes only a kind word or look."

"Well, I'll make up my mind whether or not to try it while I'm questioning the Eel," Longarm said. "And seeing as how it's going to get later before it gets any earlier, I guess I better go along and take a look at the Desert Eel, and see what sorta luck I have getting him to loosen up his jaws."

"I am sure you will not need directions to find our *carcel*," Novalo said. "There are not so many buildings for it to have escaped your notice."

Longarm shook his head. "It caught my eye right off, the only one that ain't made outa adobe."

"Putting prisoners in an adobe jail is like trying to fill a sieve with water," Novalo smiled. "I will be here through the morning, and your questioning should take only a short while. I have already sent orders to the sentry to admit you."

Standing up, Longarm replied, "I ain't going to put in

114

no more time than I need to. I oughta be back in an hour or so."

Walking through the randomly spaced buildings of the Rurale headquarters, Longarm noticed that none of the men or the few women moving around gave him more than a glance. He reached the low-set stone prison building set halfway between the headquarters and the corrals, where a sentry was lounging on the ground beside the door, his rifle leaning against the wall beside him. The man looked up as Longarm approached, but did not get to his feet until Longarm stopped in front of him.

Stretching, he asked, *"Que quiere, señor?"*

"I got to talk to one of the men you got inside there," Longarm replied. "The one you call *El Anguila del Desierto.*"

"Ah, sí. Capitan Novalo are say you are to go een."

Taking from his belt an iron ring on which several large keys dangled, the Rurale unlocked the door and pulled it open. It swung outward, a two-inch-thick wooden slab with a barred observation port in the upper section. The cool air that rushed out as it opened carried the smell of unwashed bodies and reeking slop buckets, and Longarm hoped that he would need only a short time to convince the Eel that his half-formed scheme was sound.

"Vete al derecho," the guard said. *"El Anguila del Desierto* ees een *celda* een the middle."

Longarm nodded. "I'll call you when I'm ready to leave," he told the man, and stepped into the dim, cell-lined corridor.

As the door swung closed behind him, a muttering of hushed whispers rippled along the cells, and as his eyes adjusted he saw the prisoners pressing against the bars of their doors. Longarm's eyes adjusted quickly to the dim interior, and he moved slowly down the corridor, glancing at the imprisoned men who stood looking at him as he went by. Near the center of the passageway, a voice from the cell on his right caught his attention.

"Longarm! *Madre, Dios y Santo Espiritu!* What are you doing in this place?"

Longarm's head swiveled sharply. The voice he heard was not the one he'd expected. "El Gato!" he gasped. "I guess I got to ask you the same thing!"

"Be careful of what you say!" the man in the cell warned in a lowered voice. "Some of these men are not to be trusted!"

Dropping his own voice, Longarm moved closer to the door of the cell and peered in the dim light at the man who was pressed against the barred door.

"Damned if it ain't you, all right," he whispered. "But you sure are the last man I expected to see in here, Gato!"

"And I had no idea that you would show up in such a place as this. But it is good to see you, even through bars."

Though both men spoke casually, their offhand exchange of greetings gave no clue to the bond between them. Longarm had met El Gato several years earlier while in Mexico on a case. The two had been enemies at first, until chance put them both on the same side as a matter of survival.

El Gato's nickname came from his gift of extraordinary night vision. He was the son of a rich family which had lost both wealth and possessions in an aborted revolutionary uprising. He'd moved from one guerrilla band to another, living by his wits, turning to crime when necessary to survive.

Some strange spark had been struck between him and Longarm, and though they'd met on only three previous occasions, the spark still remained. It was as though they were blood brothers, forced by circumstances to be apart, but always able to fall at once into their close relationship when chance brought them together. Just as El Gato accepted Longarm's unexpected appearance, Longarm accepted El Gato's confinement as being nothing unusual. No lengthy explanations were needed between them; they picked up the thread of their relationship at once.

116

"I was looking for *El Anguila del Desierto*, not you," Longarm said.

As though his presence in jail under a name other than his own was not unusual, El Gato replied, "Then I am the one you are here to see."

"Don't tell me you're using that alias too!"

"Only here. It was a safer name than my own to give when I was foolish enough to let the Rurales capture me."

"What about the real Eel?"

"He's dead, has been for three, maybe four months. He tried to hold up a silver shipment down in San Luis Potosí, but like the fool he was, he didn't have enough men in his bunch to handle the guards."

"Well, it looks like this is one time I'm going to have to disappoint Billy Vail," Longarm said. "He was hoping that I'd get the Eel to open up about where he hid some loot from a job or two he pulled up north of the border."

"A vain hope," El Gato replied. "When *El Anguila del Desierto* died, he took the secret of his hiding places with him."

"But how do you come to be using his name?" Longarm asked. "Don't the Rurales up here talk to the ones down where the Eel was killed?"

"There has been no change in the Rurales since you were here last, *amigo*," the prisoner said. "Each outfit goes its own way, and they are still more interested in loot than in law. I have heard stories of a group of outlaw Rurales trying to start a new revolution."

Longarm nodded. "I run into a bunch of 'em just on the other side of Ojinaga. But that ain't either here or there. You know you're supposed to stand up against the wall tomorrow morning, I guess?"

"*Seguro*. Today was to have been the day, but the *padre* who came in yesterday to give us the last rites told us that he'd persuaded that bastard Novalo to give us another day to live."

"That wasn't his idea," Longarm said. "I got into the

117

middle of the argument they was having, and showed 'em how to play a trick with the calendar so the priest could have his way."

"Me, I didn't give a damn," El Gato said. "Dead is dead, *amigo,* and one day's as bad as any other to die. But now that you're here, I'm beginning to change my mind about that."

"Well, I guess you know I wouldn't't've turned a hand to help the Eel," Longarm told his old friend. "But seeing as it's you, I don't intend for you to stand up and face that firing squad tomorrow. I ain't forgot what you done for me when I got sent down here to chop off that Laredo Loop."

"Nada de nada," El Gato said. "But I am glad you still remember me, Longarm. Now, how do you intend to get me out of here and away from the Rurales?"

"I ain't got no idea yet," Longarm admitted. "But if it comes right down to brass tacks, I'll just wait till everybody's turned in tonight, and come down here and put the guard to sleep and take his keys. I'll have my horse all saddled and one for you, and the two of us will ride for the border."

"That's as good an idea as any I've come up with," El Gata nodded. "Except for one thing. From what I've found out by watching out of my window, this place never does really go to sleep at night."

"Maybe you better tell me a little bit more," Longarm frowned. "I never seen a Rurale camp where half the men didn't go to bed too drunk to get up and walk straight, and the other half slept like they was dead."

"This is the one you haven't seen, then," El Gato said soberly. "Something happened around here a few days ago that's got the Rurales nervous as a bunch of cats."

"You got any idea what it was?"

"No. But I know that whatever happened, it sure changed things. They've got night patrols out on the grounds, and even a stray dog gets their attention. You're going to have more than just the guard at the jail door to handle."

"Now, that's something I wouldn't've noticed," Longarm frowned, "seeing as I just got here yesterday. But it might've had something to do with that bunch of outlaw Rurales I run into on my way here. They give me a bad time for a little while."

"Whatever it is, it's serious," El Gato said. "But from what I learned about you in that Laredo Loop case, if there's a way to get me out, you'll find it."

"I'm sure aiming to," Longarm nodded. "And I got all day ahead of me to look around and poke into corners and ask questions. Don't worry. You just be expecting me to open up that cell of yours sometime tonight."

"If there's anybody who can do that, it's you. And even if you should fail, I thank you now for trying, in case there is no way for me to talk to you later."

"Now, don't go borrowing trouble," Longarm told his old friend. "The day's young, and I got a lot of time to study out something."

"Do your studying, then, *amigo*. And good luck! Both of us will need it, if you're to get me out."

"You just be ready tonight," Longarm warned. "And don't let nothing surprise you, because if whatever scheme I come up with works, it can't be something that Novalo and his men'd be looking for. But you'll be outa this place before daylight, or my name ain't Custis Long!"

Chapter 12

Walking slowly back to the Rurale office, Longarm set his mind on the problem of freeing El Gato. As he moved toward the headquarters building, he studied his surroundings. There were only three main buildings: the headquarters, the jail, and the stables and the corral that adjoined them. The buildings were set well apart from one another, with wide stretches of open hard-packed ground between them. They formed an island—or, more accurately, a wide finger—that stretched back from the road. Along the perimeter of the finger on which the three main buildings stood there was a wide belt made up of tents, adobe shanties, and *jacales,* small huts built made of brush plastered with mud, where the rank and file Rurales lived with their *lavanderas*.

As he strolled, Longarm measured with his eyes the distance from the jail to the headquarters building and the stables. He scanned the area around the jail, looking for even a small bit of shelter where two men might hide in the darkness, but there was none. Wherever he looked, the situation seemed more impossible.

Longarm had known from the beginning that a daylight escape was out of the question. Even if they made it to the corrals, there was no concealing foliage in this semi-arid desert country stretching for a hundred miles in all directions.

Making a run from the camp, almost certainly with a

bunch of Rurales in pursuit, was a certain invitation to death or recapture, and Longarm had no illusions about the treatment he and El Gato would receive if they fell into the hands of the Rurales after an aborted effort to free one of their prisoners.

You just might've bit off more'n you can chew this time, old son, he mused. *But there's got to be a way to get El Gato and me outa this damn place, and there sure ain't enough time left to make no fancy plans. All you can do is bust him outa that cell and start running, and hope the devil will take the hindmost like he's supposed to, and hope the hindmost this time will be the Rurales.*

Halfway to the headquarters, Longarm saw Saffrona flouncing along on her way toward the shanties and huts. She saw him at the same time and changed her course to meet him.

"Hola, Americano," Saffrona called when she was within hearing distance. "You are go back to look for me, now you have the time? Come weeth me, then. We weel go—"

"Well, I wasn't exactly looking for you, Saffrona," Longarm replied. Even though he knew that her interest in him was more mercenary than personal, Longarm's habit of being polite to women, whether titled nobility or whores, kept him from brushing off Saffrona's second proposition of the morning. "I still got some more business to talk about with the captain."

"Que lastima!" she said, cocking her head on one side and looking at him with open interest. "I am do my work for today, so I have plenty of the time. Mebbe so when you are talk to the *capitan,* you can come see me. Or I weel go back to your room now and wait, eef you weesh."

"Trouble is, I got a lot of things to do after I get done talking to Novalo," Longarm replied. "But I thank you for the invite, anyway."

"Ees weeth me sometheeng you are not like?" she asked.

"No. I think you're a right pretty girl."

"Then why you do not say yes when I invite you? You are *mucho hombre*. When you are een bed thees morning I see that."

"I ain't got a thing against you, Saffrona," Longarm assured her. "But I just got too much business to take care of right now."

"Bah!" she snorted. Then, in a quick transformation, her scowl became a smile and she continued, "Eef you are feenish soon, you can come to find me. I weel geeve you good time."

"I bet you would, at that," he nodded. "But not now."

"Maybe later, then," Saffrona said. She pointed to one of the *jacales* which stood near the corner of the horse corral. "Ees *mi casa, ahi*. You remember eet, no?"

"I sure won't forget," Longarm promised. "Now, I got to get along. I don't want to keep Captain Novalo waiting."

Saffrona nodded and turned away with a suggestive twist of her hips, and Longarm resumed his measured walk to the headquarters. The chance encounter with Saffrona had reminded him of the half-formed idea he'd been juggling all morning.

Novalo was seated in the outer office. Behind his chair the door to the private office was ajar. He looked up from his desk when Longarm entered and lifted his thick black eyebrows as he asked, "Did you get from *El Anguila del Desierto* the information you wished?"

"No, but I ain't played my hole card yet," Longarm said. "I figure to go back and have another shot at him after he's stewed a little while longer."

"You *Norteamericanos* are too gentle with your prisoners," the Rurale snorted. "I have been thinking of this matter. If you fail, I will give the Eel to my own men. They will pull the answers out of him!"

"Oh, I could've pushed harder and made him talk," Longarm said. "But I ain't only looking for answers. I want the right ones. Something the Eel makes up just to stop somebody from hurting him ain't going to be much use to us. He's smart enough to lie to whoever's hurting him, but if we swap him something for what we want to know, it's a good chance he'll tell the truth about where his loot's hid."

"True," Novalo agreed. "You are right." He sat silently for a moment, then went on, "I am curious to know why you treat *El Anguila* with such care, and attach so much importance to the information you are after."

His question came just as Longarm fitted in the last piece of the puzzle that had been roiling around in his mind since his earlier conversation with the Rurale officer.

"I guess I better start laying my cards on the table," he said, crowding all the reluctance he could muster into his voice. "Ever since my chief told me about the Eel up in Denver, I been trying to figure things out so I'll get what's rightly coming to me. I guess I got to start out by explaining that we don't do things on our side of the border like you do here."

"I am aware of this," Novalo nodded. "You do not need to explain, Long."

"I better, though, just to make sure you understand," Longarm went on. "Now, when you Rurales take a prisoner that's got a bunch of his loot stowed away, you don't have to hand it over. You keep it for yourself."

"You are making my Rurales sound as bad as the thieves we bring in," Novalo protested. "We do nothing that is against our country's laws."

"That ain't what I said," Longarm pointed out. "Take the Desert Eel, now. I was sent down here because he knows where the loot from two big jobs he pulled in Texas is tucked away."

"And you wished to recover it, of course," Novalo nodded.

"Them's the orders I got from my chief," Longarm nodded. "Now, besides the money the Eel got when he stuck up the Overland Mail and I guess some other places, too, there's a reward on him put up by the U. S. government for killing a post-office clerk that was in the mail car of a train he held up."

"This I already know," Novalo nodded. "The papers Morales turned over to me have that information in them."

"Well, now," Longarm said, leaning forward in his chair, "I done all the work running down the Eel and arresting him, but there's a law in our country that says I can't take a penny of the reward money, just because the government pays me wages."

"I have not heard of this," the Rurale said, leaning forward in his chair. "Your government is miserly, no?"

"You can bet a plugged dollar to a double eagle it is!" Longarm agreed. "And there's another reward the railroad's put up for whoever brings in the Eel, but on account of I work for the government, I can't collect any of that, either."

Novalo shook his head sympathetically. "You are indeed being shabbily treated, my friend."

"That's why I done some figuring," Longarm went on. "And that's why I been so anxious to catch up with the Eel. You see, Novalo, he's put away all the loot he stole, hid it out someplace, and if I can worm out of him where he's hid it, I figure that because I ain't getting any of the reward money, I'm entitled to hold onto the loot."

"Ah!" Novalo nodded. "Now I see why yesterday you were so quick to find a way to keep the condemned prisoners alive! You wished to talk with *El Anguila!* You do not want to go away with empty pockets, no?"

"Well, just put yourself in my place," Longarm suggested. "Would you feel you was getting a fair shake?"

"Most certainly not!" the Rurale exclaimed. "You are being treated most unfairly, my friend. A man must look after his own interests, and refuse to let others cheat him of what should be his reward for hard work and danger."

124

Longarm nodded. "I sorta figured that's the way you'd look at it."

"It is the only fair way to consider the matter," Novalo said. He thought for a moment, then asked, "This loot from *El Anguila's* robberies, do you know how much it amounts to?"

"I ain't got no exact figures, but it's got to add up to a pretty sizeable chunk of money. I heard that since he's got away, he's pulled quite a few jobs down on this side of the border."

"His hoard is hidden in Mexico?"

"Oh, I reckon he's got a little bit hid someplace, but the money I know about is on the other side of the border. That's why I figured I better talk to you first."

"For what reason?" Novalo frowned. "We settled the matter between us before you talked to *El Anguila*. What else is there to discuss?"

"I'd say quite a lot," Longarm answered. "Why, I ain't even told you yet what I got in mind."

"Then suppose you do so, even though I think I have a good idea of what you will propose."

"That's what I come here for," Longarm went on. "Now, you can collect the rewards that the U. S. government's got out on the Eel, but I can't. I can find out where his loot's hid, but you can't, so—"

"Hold on," Novalo broke in. "Do not be so sure, Long! I have just learned from you for the first time of *El Anguila's* hoard of treasures. Now that I know of it, it will be a very easy thing for me to persuade him to tell where his stolen money is hidden."

"I wouldn't be too sure of that, Captain Novalo," Longarm said quietly. "I sized up the Eel while I was talking to him. He ain't the kind of man that'd talk easy and if your men shoot him before he tells me where that loot is hid, there ain't much chance of nobody finding it."

"I have my ways," Novalo said in a toneless voice. His

implied threat was more sinister than it might have been if he'd spoken loudly. He added, "This *Anguila* would not be the first one my men and I have persuaded to reveal a secret."

"Well, I guess that'd be up to you," Longarm told Novalo. "But there's some things you might think about."

"What are these things?"

"One is that you ain't heard my proposition yet. That's the biggest one. I'll just keep my mouth shut about the rest for right now, until I see whether or not you're going along."

"Tell me your proposition, then," Novalo said.

"Before I go any further, there's two or three things you need to be thinking about," Longarm said.

"I am listening," Novalo nodded.

"Now, the way I figure it, the Eel was running pretty hard when I was put on his trail after he robbed that mail train. He didn't have time to spend much money, but he had plenty of time to hide it. And wherever he hid it along his trail, I'd know just about where to look."

"Then you think there is a great deal of money hidden from the train robbery?"

"I'd come real close to staking my badge on it. And once I've pried out of him where he hid it, it ain't going to take me long to find it. Now, was you to go hunting it, you might spend a year and never even get close, because you don't know your way around that neck of the woods like I do."

"That is a point worth considering," Novalo said. "One that had not occurred to me."

"Now, the way I've studied it out, them other jobs the Eel pulled before he ducked back into Mexico was close enough to where he'd hid the loot from the train robbery for him to put all of it together. I'll know about that before I finish talking to him tonight, but I doubt he'd tell you."

"Go on to the next point you wish to make," Novalo said.

"I'd sorta like to know what your bosses in the Rurales might get to thinking if you asked 'em to give you time off to go rambling around up north of the Rio Grande. Was I them, I'd get a mite suspicious."

"A minor point, but well taken," Novalo agreed.

"I guess the other thing that come to mind is what you'd call minor, too," Longarm said. "But I'd sure like to know how you figure to go rambling all over the countryside north of the Rio Grande without drawing an awful lot of attention."

"It would be difficult, but not impossible." Novalo frowned. "But let us go to the real meat. Exactly what do you propose?"

"You collect the reward money that's on the Eel's head. The government'll pay it to you, but not to me. I'll find out from the Eel where he's hid his take. We'll put the reward money and whatever he stole together, and split it down the middle, half for you and half for me."

"I might have to pass some of my share on to some of my men, if they give me help in getting it."

"Not if you do it my way," Longarm countered. "As long as there's just the two of us in this thing, we can keep it quiet."

"You think well, Long," Novalo nodded.

"And you might do some thinking, too, if what you got in the back of your mind is trying to cut me out of a fair split," Longarm said. "Suppose you and your men was to go out and start beating the Eel to get him to talk. Even if he did talk, you figure he'd tell you the truth?"

Novalo sat in thoughtful silence for a few seconds. Then he nodded and said, "You have a point there, Long. But why would he not lie to you as quickly as he would to me?"

"Because I'd be giving him something he'd like to have, and you'd just be hurting him," Longarm shot back.

"What could you give him that I could not?"

"I'd be a plumb fool to tell you that, now wouldn't I?"

Smiling thinly, the Rurale nodded. "Yes. But even if I am sure I know what you propose to offer, I can see the truth in what you have said."

"Have we got a deal, then?"

"We have a deal," Novalo agreed.

"And no cheating?" Longarm insisted.

"No. You have my word on it. Now, tell me how you propose to get *El Anguila* to talk."

Though Longarm had no doubt that Novalo's promise was worth about as much as a handful of air, he'd gone too far now to back away. He said, "You was right about it being easy to figure out what I aim to do. We talked about it earlier. I guess you know a *lavandera* that calls herself Saffrona?"

"Of course. She sweeps and dusts the headquarters rooms."

"Well, I ain't going to ask you if you know anything more about her, but I got a hunch she does a little bit more than sweep and dust. Anyhow, I'm going to get her to walk by the jail, where the Eel can get a good look at her, and tell him she's his for the night if he opens up and tells me whereabouts he's hid his loot."

"And you think he'll tell you the truth?" Novalo asked skeptically.

"Well, now, Captain, I'd guess you've questioned a pretty fair number of prisoners in your job. I know I have, and I can tell pretty fast whether a man's lying to me or not."

"True," Novalo agreed. "There is a way they hold their head, the way their hands move, the tone of their voice."

Longarm nodded. "That's what I was getting at. And I've found out something else, too. The closer a man is to dying, the easier it is for him to come out with the truth."

"There is something in that, too," Novalo said. "Very well. I suppose you will want me to order the man on night sentry duty at the jail to let you bring the girl in?"

"No, sir!" Longarm exclaimed vehemently. "That's the

last thing I want you to do! I'll get your man outa the way without hurting him too bad. Just leave that to me."

"Agreed," Novalo nodded. Then he said thoughtfully, "There is one more thing that occurs to me, Marshal Long."

"What's that?" Longarm asked.

"A somewhat delicate subject," Novalo shrugged. "You and I have no reason to trust one another. What is to prevent me from breaking my promise to you, or to prevent you from breaking your promise to me?"

"Just one thing," Longarm said, his voice barely above a whisper, but as hard as a plate of tempered steel.

"And what is that?"

"When I leave that jail tonight, the Eel's going to be a dead man. And I don't much like what I'll have to do, but if that little *lavandera* gets a chance to hear what me and the Eel talks about, she's going to be dead, too. And I'll be the only one that knows where the Eel's loot is hid."

"Again, I do not give you enough credit." Novalo smiled, a thin-lipped, evil smile. "You speak like one of my veteran Rurales. The only silent witness is a dead one."

"Just a minute," Longarm said, his voice as steely as it had been before. "I ain't done yet. I'll just give you one more thing to think about."

"Go ahead."

"When I step outa that jail tonight, I'll be the only man in the world that knows where the Eel's loot is hid. Now, I'd just imagine that loot is worth three or four times as much as them rewards you'll be getting. I don't think you're going to be stupid enough to try getting rid of me, not before you've seen how much the whole bundle adds up to."

"You have nothing to worry about, Marshal Long," Novalo said. "I understand exactly what you are saying. If any harm comes to you tonight, it will not be of my planning. You have my word on that."

"Well, since you stand to make a good-sized pile of

money by keeping me from getting shot full of holes, I guess I'm safe in taking your word, Captain Novalo. So unless you got something else to talk about, we got a deal."

"I think we have covered everything, Long," Novalo said. "We do indeed have a deal."

"I'll be moving along, then," Longarm said. "I'll find a way to let you know when the time comes for us to split the money up. Now, there's a lot of things I got to take care of, and there ain't much time left in the day for me to do 'em, so I'll just mosey along and get busy."

Chapter 13

Longarm took his time as he started across the two- or three-acre plot of bare ground over which the buildings of the Rurale headquarters sprawled. By now the sun was high in the sky, climbing towards noon, and the air had gotten warm. The heat wasn't uncomfortable yet, though he knew that within another two hours or less it would reach the stage when wise men stayed indoors.

Walking slowly and flicking his eyes from side to side as he studied his surroundings in light of the plan he'd made, Longarm moved steadily away from the road toward the vee of small houses and shacks which lined the headquarters area.

Near the center of the area of well-beaten earth which surrounded all three of the buildings that formed the headquarters, he stopped to light a cheroot. While his head was bent forward, his hands cupping the match, he made a half-turn before dropping the match he held and taking out another. While he was puffing for the second time his eyes were busy gauging distances.

Moving on at last, trailing blue cigar smoke behind him, he turned and continued his slow pacing, memorizing the distances between the stables and corral at the rear, the jail which sat at an angle to one side, and the headquarters building which formed the third corner of the flattened triangle made by the three structures.

He did not like what he saw. The distances between the

buildings were too great to be crossed quickly, even on horseback, and in many brushes with the Rurales, Long-arm had learned that while they lacked the spit-and-polished looks of American Army cavalry, they reacted quickly to emergencies and fought fiercely.

Approximately in the center of the triangle was the well, almost equally distant from the three major buildings. The headquarters building was nearest the road which ran past the installation, the jail formed one apex of the triangle, the barn and corrals beyond it made the third point.

On all three sides there were tents, *jacales* and small one-room adobe houses. These were occupied by the Rurales and their families and the *lavanderas*. The ramshackle little structures were scattered in a belt of a hundred or more yards wide, flanking the open area of well-beaten earth surrounding the buildings. The fringe created by the shanties extended from the road to the end of the triangle on one side and back up the other sides to the road again.

Longarm eyed the mixture of small dwellings as he headed for the corral. There were two basic types of them. One kind had been cobbled together from five-gallon oil cans which had originally contained kerosene; the cans had been converted into metal sheets by cutting away the tops and bottoms and flattening the sides, then the sheets nailed over a wooden framework.

A few of them were more elaborate. These actually could be called houses, for they had been made from adobe bricks. None of them was large—basically each was just one big room—and their low, flat roofs were very little higher than a man's head. Perhaps one in every dozen of the adobes had glass windows and wooden doors, but in most of them open holes served.

At a glance, the *jacales* could have been mistaken for adobe houses, but a close second look would have shown that they were quite different. The more substantial of them were made by plastering a layer of adobe mud over a framework of sticks or branches. Lacking any supporting timbers, the walls of many of them had sagged inward, throwing the entire structure out of plumb. Few of these had walls sturdy enough to allow a window to be cut into them, and in most the door was a low triangular opening.

As for the tents, they were even more varied than the *jacales*. Here and there Longarm saw some which had been made of brown or white canvas, but these made only a few dots among the others. A majority of the tents had tops and sides that looked like patchwork quilts, for they had been pieced together from fabrics of all types, textures, and colors.

There was no such thing as streets or paths in the settlement that bordered the three headquarters buildings. The huts and *jacales* and adobe structures might have been tossed from a giant fist and left in the places where they landed willy-nilly. As he walked away from the Rurale headquarters and surveyed the untidy settlement that surrounded it on three sides, Longarm shook his head.

Old son, he told himself, *there ain't no way at all to guide a couple of horses through them shanties in the dark. If you was to try to do that, you'd rouse the whole damn place. But if you was to open them corrals back there and chase the horses out just before starting to get away, they'd raise so much commotion that you'd be able to ride fast through that clear space to the road. That'd give you and El Gato a five- or six-mile start on the Rurales, and with that much of a lead, you and El Gato sure oughta be able to beat 'em to the Rio Grande.*

Longarm had marked in memory the *jacal* to which Saffrona had pointed during their brief conversation earlier in the day. It was like those around it, a framework of wood plastered over with adobe, doorless and windowless. He stopped at the door and tapped lightly on the edge of the opening. Saffrona's face popped through the dark triangle. She was smiling as she gazed at him.

"So you are find time to veesit weeth me, now," she said. "Come inside."

133

"I didn't come here for what you got in mind, Saffrona," Longarm said as the girl moved aside and he bent almost double to go through the low doorway. Saffrona was sitting on a pallet, two or three quilts folded to serve as a mattress and a blanket spread over them. He went on, "But I'll make it worth your while to listen to me a minute or so, and if you take me up on the proposition I got in mind to make you, you'll get paid a lot more."

"What ees thees you mean, pro-po-seetion?" she asked, a small frown wrinkling her arched brow. "I theenk I know all the ways a man eenjoys, but thees I do not hear of yet."

"It ain't what you think it is," Longarm assured her. He was inside the *jacal* by now, bending almost double to keep his head from going through the conical roof. "I don't guess you'll mind me setting down by you? If I got to bend over like this much longer, I'm gonna get a crick in my back."

"Seet down," she said, moving to make room for him beside her on the pallet. "I weel listen to what you say. But first, you must tell me what I am to call you. I know you are of the United States *federalista policia,* but thees ees all."

"Well, my name's Long, but I got a sorta nickname that I answer to better. It's Longarm."

"Long-arm," she repeated, making it into two words. "Ees good. We are to be friends, no?"

"Well, I'm hoping we will be. Now let's talk, Saffrona."

Longarm fumbled in his pocket and fished out a quarter-eagle. He held it for Saffrona to see the profile of the Indian wearing a feather headdress. She reached at once for the coin, but he closed his big hand around it.

"I imagine you know better'n I do what this is worth in Mexican money," he said. "Something like five *pesos,* if I recall rightly."

She nodded.

"I don't suppose you get anything that much for making

beds and cleaning up the Rurales' office, do you?"

Saffrona snorted contemptuously. "Ees one *peso* each month. For thees I clean and sleep weeth *Capitan* Novalo two, three nights een week."

"I'll give you this gold piece just to get you to listen to me while I tell you about the job I got in mind," Longarm continued. "But it ain't just to pay you for listening. You got to guarantee me that you'll keep quiet about what I want you to do if you turn down my proposition."

"You are pay me jus' to leesten while you talk?" Saffrona asked incredulously. "I don' have to do for you notheeng?"

"That's right," he assured her. "I'll pay you for just listening and keeping your mouth shut later on. And if you take on the job, I'll give you two more coins just like this one when it's done. That's a lot of money, and what I want you to do is only going to take an hour or so."

"What ees thees job?" she frowned. "Two times now you are say 'job.' Eet must be very *importante* eef you pay so much to do eet."

"It's important, and maybe even dangerous," Longarm nodded. "And I got to ask you to promise me you won't talk about it, even if you don't take it on."

"Es *secreto*, no?" She frowned, her face serious now.

Longarm nodded. "It's real secret. It'll make the captain and the Rurales mad, and if you do it you'd best get away from here as soon as it's done. If they was to find out you'd helped me, they'd likely hurt you, or even kill you."

Saffrona sat silent for a moment, and Longarm could see that she was thinking about what he'd said. At last she shrugged and shook her head.

"Ees a great deal of money you are talk about," she said thoughtfully. "Weeth eet, I can go to Ciudad Chihuahua, even Torreon, maybe Monterey. The Rurales do not go to such beeg places, so there ees leetle danger that they weel find me." She held out her hand for the coin. "I weel listen to what you want me to do."

135

"And you won't tell anybody what we'll be talking about, even if you don't take on the job?" Longarm asked.

"I weel say notheeng. I do not owe to the Rurales anytheeng at all."

"Good." He nodded, putting the gold coin in Saffrona's hand. "Now, what I want you to do is put on two sets of clothes tonight. I'll come back here for you after dark, and take you to the jail. There's a prisoner in there called *El Anguila del Desierto*. I reckon you've heard the Rurales talking about him?"

Saffrona nodded. "I am hear *Capitan* Morales and *Capitan* Novalo talk much of heem."

"All right," Longarm continued. "He'll be waiting for you, and he'll know what to do."

"Eef he does not know, I weel show him," she said.

"What you and him is going to do ain't what you're thinking about, Saffrona," Longarm said quickly. "You give him one set of the clothes you got on. By the time he's dressed, I'll have the jailer outa commission. I'll get his keys and unlock the jailhouse doors, and let the two of you out, and put the jailer in the cell *El Anguila* was in. Then him and me will mount up and ride off, and you come on back here to your house and go to sleep like you never went outside all night."

Saffrona sat silently for a long moment. Then she shook her head slowly and said, "I cannot do thees thing."

"You mean you're afraid to?"

"Hmph!" she snorted. "I do not have afraid to go een jail, thees I do sometimes when prisoner want woman and can pay. But weel see me the Rurale who ees guard jail, he ees tell *Capitan* Novalo. Then when they find the prisoner ees escape, I weel be shoot, or maybe worse."

"Worse?" Longarm frowned.

"I am see one time, *Capitan* Novalo he ees put woman who do not please heem to *el chingo del caballo*. She ees leev only leetle while when horse ees fenesh, but—" Saffrona shook her head. "No. Ees not much I have, but even

136

eef you pay me more I weel not do thees."

Longarm had not counted on such a firm and flat refusal. He sat silently in the dimness, trying to think of another way to get El Gato out of jail and a safe distance away before his escape was discovered, but nothing came to mind. He went back to his original scheme, turning it over and looking for flaws. Then in a flash the answer came to him.

"Saffrona," he said. "Would you do this job if me and *El Anguila* take you with us when we go?"

Now it was Saffrona's turn to think. She sat for a moment or two with her full lower lip clenched between her teeth, her eyes focused on the opposite wall of the little hut. When Longarm was just about to interrupt her thinking and ask for a reply, she nodded.

"I weel do it," she said. "I theenk you are more smart as *Capitan* Novalo."

"You're sure you got enough clothes to give a dress or skirt to *El Anguila*? And maybe one of them scarves like you ladies down here in Mexico wear over your head?"

"I have all we weel need. I am breeng dress and *rebozo*."

"And you think we can make it outa here free and clear after we get *El Anguila* outa the jailhouse?"

"Como no?" she shrugged. "Ees good *eschema*. Now, you are fecnesh tell to me what I am to do, we can—"

"Not now, Saffrona," Longarm interrupted. "But don't worry. Since you're going with me and *El Anguila,* we'll find a time and place to get together."

Saffrona turned down the corners of her lips and shrugged, then said, "When you are want me to go to *el cuartel?*"

"I'll come for you just as soon as things settle down for the night," he said. "You be ready, now, because I don't aim to wait long after Novalo goes to bed."

Saffrona nodded. "I weel be ready."

As he walked back toward the jail, Longarm frowned

thoughtfully, wondering now if, after having overlooked the obvious matter of securing Saffrona's safety after he and the Eel had gone, he might not have left another gaping hole in his hastily conceived scheme.

That's what the trouble is with making plans in a hurry, old son, he told himself as he looked at the corral just ahead and the jail and headquarters building beyond them. *When you got to come up with a scheme in a hurry, you're liable to miss something important. Now, we'll need horses tonight, so you just better go look at them nags in the corral, and see if you can spot two that ain't spavined or walking lame.*

There were eight or ten horses in the pole corral, including Longarm's cavalry remount. The sturdy roan was almost two hands higher at the shoulder than the smaller, more compactly built Mexican ponies, and seemed to be in excellent shape. After watching the animals for a moment or so, he selected two that seemed the most likely looking, stored their markings away in his mind, and went on toward the jail.

Luckily, the jailer who'd admitted him earlier in the day was still on duty. The man opened the heavy door without asking any questions, and Longarm walked along the dismal corridor. El Gato had been lying against the wall under the foot-square barred window near the ceiling which let in barely enough light to allow facial features to be distinguished.

"I didn't expect to see you back so soon, *amigo*," El Gato said. "What kind of news do you have for me, good or bad?"

"Right now it looks pretty good, but don't count on it staying that way," Longarm told him. "Listen careful, now, so you won't get surprised by what's apt to happen tonight."

"You have a good plan?"

"I made the best one I could in the time I had."

"Let me hear it, then," El Gato suggested. "I am curious

to know how you expect the two of us to escape from sixty or more Rurales."

"First off," Longarm began, "I'll be back here tonight soon as Novalo goes to bed. There's a girl from the shantytown back of the corral that I got to get and bring with me."

"Even looking at a girl would be enjoyable, Longarm," El Gato smiled. "But do you think this is the time and place for us to have a party?"

"Damn it, stop joshing me!" Longarm told his friend. "This girl's your ticket outside. Her name's Saffrona, and she's one of the *lavanderas*, but we need her help!"

"Go on, then. I promise, no more jokes."

Longarm said, "Now, from what I seen, the people in them shanties don't keep real regular hours, so Saffrona's going to bring you a dress to put on."

"Please, Longarm!" El Gato protested. "I will feel like a fool wearing the clothes of a woman!"

"What'd you rather be, a live fool or a dead wise man?" Longarm asked him. "There's sentries posted at the road and there's always some of the Rurales that live in the shantytown rambling around at all hours, from what I seen of 'em since I been here."

Still grinning, El Gato nodded. "Go on, I am listening."

"Soon as you got the dress on, you and Saffrona walk down to the corral. I'll need time to get three horses saddled up, so you don't have to be in a hurry. We'll mount up and ride slow and easy up to the road and then put the boot to the horses and head for the Rio Grande."

El Gato was silent for several moments after Longarm stopped speaking. Then in a voice tinged with worry, he asked, "And that is all of your plan?"

"That's all. Why?"

"It's easy to see that you have not broken out of as many jails as I have, *amigo,*" El Gato replied. "When one prisoner escapes, it sets the others into turmoil. They shout and yell and strike the bars of the cells. The Rurales are not fools. They act very quickly indeed."

"Oh, I ain't taking 'em to be fools," Longarm replied. "But I figure the first thing they'd do is hit up on a run for the headquarters building."

El Gato shook his head. "The Rurales will be moving before we can get from the corral to the road. No, we must find some way to keep the prisoners quiet, or we will not even get out of the corral before the Rurales will be shooting at us."

"That sure wouldn't help us none, seeing they outnumber us about twenty to one," Longarm frowned. "About the only bunch that's on our side is these fellows here in jail with you, and I ain't so sure I'd trust them in a pinch."

"We have nothing to lose by trying," El Gato said. "They know they are dead men, no matter what happens. Wait." He moved to the door of the cell and for the next few minutes Longarm tried vainly to follow the rapid exchange of fast-spoken Spanish between El Gato and the prisoners. At last El Gato turned away from the door, nodding in satisfaction.

"They will help," he said. "I thought they might, since they have nothing to lose. They want you to give them the gun you will take from the jailer, and any other weapons you can find for them. Then they will provide a diversion by drawing the Rurales here to the jail while we reach the road."

"There ain't no way I can see to get 'em any more guns," Longarm frowned. "And I figured on the jailer's gun for you. I sure ain't going to give 'em my Colt or my Winchester, but you can use whichever one of 'em you want."

"If your scheme works, we will need only the guns you have," El Gato said. "When will you come to start our plan?"

"If we're going to stay ahead of the Rurales that'll be chasing us, we'll need the dark to cover us," Longarm said. "I figure we better move as soon as this place settles down for the night. If we can get just a couple of miles' lead before the Rurales start after us, we oughta be able to beat 'em to the Rio Grande. And once we're on the other side of the river, we'll be home, free and clear."

Chapter 14

"Marshal Long!" Novalo called as he saw Longarm passing the door of his office. "We must talk at once!"

"What's on your mind, Captain?" Longarm asked, turning and going into the office.

"I am very interested in finding out which of your plans you propose to use to get my prisoner to talk to you," Novalo said. "The day is passing. I am sure you have not forgotten that tomorrow morning at dawn, my firing squad will take *El Anguila* and the other prisoners to the execution wall."

"Oh, I ain't forgetting. Right now it looks like it's gonna be sorta touch and go, though," Longarm said.

"You have had trouble? *El Anguila* is refusing to tell you anything?"

"Now, don't go getting upset, Captain. You ain't got a thing to worry about. I got the Eel all primed to talk, soon as I make good on my promise to fix him up with a woman tonight."

"And you have one for him?"

Longarm nodded. "Right after supper. I'll give him till midnight to have his last fling. Then, when I go in to get her outa his cell, he's swore he'll tell me the places where all his loot's hid."

"This woman, she will not know why you are taking her to a prisoner?"

"Now, you don't think I'd be fool enough to spread the

word to anybody else about what's really going on, do you?"

Novalo said thoughtfully, "No. You do not appear to me as a man who would make such a mistake."

"Then just stop worrying," Longarm said.

"From what you say, I am sure our plan will work!" Novalo exclaimed, his face twisting in a wolfish grin. "Now we must complete it. I will have to learn from you what formalities I must go through to claim my reward for capturing *El Anguila*."

"That ain't going to be such a much of a job," Longarm assured him. "Soon as I get back to Denver, I'll tell my chief you got the money coming to you, and he'll take care of the rest. You'll get it soon as the Treasury Department hands it over."

Greed written on his face, Novalo asked, "This place, Denver, that you speak of, is it far north of the border?"

"It's a right good piece. About as far as we are now from Mexico City. But if you're thinking about going all the way to Washington to ask for it, that's a real long trip."

"Perhaps I should request a leave from my post," Novalo frowned. "It would be more satisfactory to have the money paid to me instead of it passing through other hands. And there is also the matter of you recovering what *El Anguila* has hidden. I would like to go with you to the place where it is hidden."

Longarm checked his rising temper and kept his voice mild as he said slowly, "You know, it sounds to me like you got an idea that either Billy Vail or me, or maybe both of us, is going to try to cheat you."

"Such a thing was not in my mind!" Novalo protested. "I was only thinking of the convenience it would be for you and your chief marshal if I relieved you of the job of transferring the money to me!"

"Well, you suit yourself about what you want to do to collect, Captain. Any way you feel like working it out will be fine with me. But I feel like we better wait till after I

143

talk to the Eel tonight before we start talking about divvy-ing up."

"Of course," Novalo said hastily. "But if your scheme is successful, we must give thought to such matters as I have mentioned. You will agree that they concern us both."

"Oh, sure," Longarm nodded. "But the eggs ain't going to be hatched out for a while, so let's don't go counting the chickens too quick. Now, I better move along. I got a lot of work to do tonight, and I'd sorta like to take a little *siesta* before I start."

Back in his temporary headquarters, Longarm stretched out on the bed and propped his shoulders up on the head-board. With a cigar in one hand and the bottle of Tom Moore in the other, he alternated sips with puffs while he reviewed his plans.

By the time he'd gone through all the details twice, he was finally satisfied. Snuffing out the cigar butt, he replaced the cork in the bottle, then slid down until his head was resting on the pillow and went to sleep.

As it always did, Longarm's mental alarm clock woke him at the time he'd set it to get up, when the sun was begin-ning to dip low for its final plunge behind the horizon. He studied the distorted rectangle cast on the wall by its red-dening rays and decided that the time had come for him to move.

Swinging his feet to the floor, he cleared his throat with a small swallow of Tom Moore, then methodically checked his Winchester and Colt. Emptying the rifle's magazine, he applied tiny droplets of oil to the hinge-screws of its lever, trigger, and hammer, and wiped away the excess before reloading. A spin of the Colt's cylinder told him that it needed no oiling, but he tested its hammer's action before restoring the well-used pistol to its holster.

Packing his saddlebags, he took a blanket off the bed and spread it on the floor. He then put the bags and rifle in the blanket's center and folded and overlapped the edges to make a rough parcel of them. Taking out his pocketknife, he cut strips from the blanket's edge and tied the parcel, leaving one long strip dangling. Using this strip as a handle, Longarm picked up the bundle and lowered it carefully out the window until it came to rest on the ground.

Leaning out, Longarm lifted the bundle until it swung clear and started swinging it back and forth along the building's side. When he released his grip, the elongated parcel was at the point where it fell against the wall. The dun-colored blanket blended with the dun-colored ground in a manner that made it almost invisible.

Satisfied that he'd taken all the precautions possible, Longarm left the headquarters building and made his way to Saffrona's *jacal*. By the time he reached it, the sun had set and the blue of night was creeping across the eastern sky.

"We are ready to play our leetle game, no?" she greeted him.

"I am if you are, Saffrona. But don't get no ideas about this being a game. If something goes wrong, if you or me make a mistake, we might find ourselves up against a wall looking down a firing squad's rifle barrels."

"Thees I would not like. But do not worry, Longarm. I weel be careful."

"Have you got on two dresses, like I told you to wear?" he asked, looking at her and seeing no sign that she wore two complete outfits.

"Seguro. I am do what you say."

"And you're sure you know what we're going to do?"

"Sin duda," she nodded. "I am sure."

Longarm glanced outside and saw the twilight had begun. "We might as well start out, then. I got my own little jobs to take care of while you're in with the Eel, and they'll be easier to handle if I can see what I'm doing."

"Bueno," Saffrona nodded. *"Vaminos ahora mismo."*

Side by side they began weaving their way between the higgledy-piggledy huts and hovels. By the time they

reached the jail the twilight was noticeably deeper. The
sentry on duty at the jail was the same one who'd been on
guard during Longarm's earlier visits. He glanced at Saffrona with open admiration, and nodded to Longarm.

"*Capitan* Novalo ees tell me you are to breeng woman
for the preesoner you talk at," he said. "I weel put her een
cell weeth *El Anguila del Desierto*."

"Fine," Longarm replied. "After she's in there, just
leave 'em alone till I get back. I won't be gone but a little
while."

Without waiting to watch the guard and Saffrona enter
the building, Longarm turned away. Through the gathering
darkness he started walking with long strides toward the
headquarters. A light shone through the door of Novalo's
office and the captain was still at his desk when Longarm
went in. Novalo looked up from the paper he'd been studying.

"You have arranged everything we agreed, I hope?" he
asked.

"I done the best I could," Longarm nodded. "The
woman's in with the Eel now. Give him a night with her
and he'll tell me where his loot's hid away." Then, hardening his voice in a manner that he was sure would strike a
responsive cord in the Rurale's mind, he added, "I might
have to persuade him a little bit if he tries to beg off, but
you and me both know that a man can only stand so much
before he gives in."

"Perhaps I had better go with you when you return,"
Novalo suggested. "I have had some experience in extract-
ing words from stubborn prisoners."

Shaking his head, Longarm said, "That don't strike me
as being such a good idea, captain. The Eel ain't got no
love for you and your Rurales. If you was to show up with
me, he'd shut up like a clam, and I misdoubt we'd get a
word outa him."

"You may be right," Novalo agreed after he'd thought

this over for a moment. "We will proceed as we had planned, then."

Longarm nodded. "It'll be better if we do." He stood up. "Now, I got a real long night ahead of me. I'm going to grab a few minutes of shuteye, then I'll mosey back on out to the jail and finish up my job."

Longarm wasted little time in his room. He pulled the thin pillows into the center of the bed, arranged them end-to-end lengthwise, and covered them with the bed's second blanket. The elongated shape he created was crude and clumsy, but when he blew out the lamp and inspected it in the room's darkness the bundle looked enough like a man to fool someone who glanced in casually. He levered himself out of the window and dropped to the ground, then picked up the blanket-swathed bundle containing his rifle and saddlebags and made his way through the darkness to the corral.

As early as the night was, many inhabitants of the shanty-town surrounding the Rurale headquarters were already going to bed. Cooking-fires still burned in front of a number of the makeshift dwellings, though most of them were being allowed to die, and the glows from their dying coals created very little light. Lamps and lanterns glowed yellow through the windows of several of the adobe huts, but there were very few people moving around. Some-where in the distance a lone guitarist was plucking chords from his instrument, and there were a few voices raised in argument or discussions here and there among the shanties.

Longarm kept to the perimeter of the settlement, out of the dimly lighted margin created by the few fires that were still burning. Now and then he passed a *jacal* where some-one stood outside, and occasionally he encountered some-one else, usually a man, who was walking through the zone of semi-darkness. A few of those within speaking distance greeted him, and he replied with a *hola* or *tarde* of his own.

147

At the corral, the darkness was almost complete, but by now his eyes had adjusted and there was enough light spilling from the dying cooking-fires of the nearest dwellings to allow him to pick out his cavalry mount. When he had scouted the stable area earlier, Longarm had noticed that the Rurales had a habit of tossing bits of harness over the corral rails and leaving them there to be handy the next morning. After a few minutes of exploration with his fingers along the rails he found the two hackamores he would need, and ducked between the rails into the corral.

Even in the darkness, Longarm had no trouble locating his cavalry mount. The gelding was almost a hand higher at the shoulders than most of the Mexican horses. He slid the hackamore over the horse's head and led it to the corner of the corral nearest the stable, where he tethered it with a pull-knot that would slip open at a quick tug. Then he set out to locate the two animals he'd spotted during his earlier visit, and within a quarter of an hour he was able to lead all three of the animals into the stable and still have a hand free to carry the bundle containing his rifle and saddlebags.

With the roof of the stable cutting off the starshine and its walls shielding the interior from the faint trickle of light that still glowed from the dying fires, locating his own McClellan saddle was more time-consuming than he'd thought it would be. He groped along the tops of the chest-high partitions between the stalls for what seemed to him an interminably long time before his fingers encountered the familiar well-rubbed leather, but once he'd found the saddle he made short work of putting it on the cavalry horse.

After his own mount was ready and tethered to a post by the stable door, Longarm's job became easier. There was plenty of gear to choose from, and though the saddling itself was a job of feeling and fumbling in the blackness of the stable's interior, he made a reasonably fast job of securing saddles to the other two horses. Tethering them beside the cavalry horse, he opened the stable door enough to let him slide through to the open.

After the deep darkness of the stable, the starshine and the dim glows from the few fast-fading fires that still glowed beyond the corrals made the night seem almost as bright as the after-sunset glow had been an hour or two earlier. Longarm stood motionless for a few moments, his eyes flickering across the area around him.

There were fewer lights showing through windows of the shanties now. Occasionally one of these was blotted out as some homeward-bound resident passed it, but the guitarist had given up, and the vague undercurrent of noise that always arises from an inhabited area had died to a whisper. Longarm's fingers moved almost automatically to his vest pocket for a cigar. He had the long slim cylinder between his teeth and was reaching for a match before he became aware of what he was doing. Shaking his head at his thoughtlessness, he returned the cigar to his vest pocket and started toward the jail.

"Quien pase?" the jailer challenged when he heard Longarm's bootsoles scraping the bare ground.

Sure that the man would recognize his voice by now, Longarm replied, "Don't get all excited. I just come to get the girl and talk to the prisoner, like I said I would."

"Ah!" the man said. *"El mariscal Americano. 'Sta bueno.* I am not see who you are een the dark."

By now Longarm was only a few steps away. As he closed the distance between himself and the jailer, he went on, "I got to talk to the Eel a minute or two. I don't guess you'd mind me going along with you? You can bring the girl outside, and I'll take her off your hands soon as I wind up my business with the Eel."

"'Sta bueno," the jailer replied. *"Acompañame."*

Turning, the jailer selected the doorkey from his ring and fumbled it into the keyhole. Longarm stepped up, drawing his Colt. Before the jailer could finish turning the key, Longarm swept the revolver down in a clubbing blow that crumpled the man's high-crowned hat and landed with a thud on his skull. The jailer was unconscious even before he started slumping to the ground.

Longarm stepped up quickly and caught the falling man before he could hit the ground. Supporting the limp form with one muscular arm, he finished turning the key and pulled the door open. Dragging the jailer with him, he stepped inside.

Though the cool evening air had lessened the stench of the jail's interior, the smell was still strong. Longarm let the jailer down in the corridor and stepped quickly up to El Gato's cell as he holstered his Colt. He could see nothing in the blackness, but he heard the murmur of voices in the cells along the corridor and knew that speed was essential. He moved quickly to the center cell.

"Gato!" he whispered.

"I am ready, *amigo,*" El Gato replied instantly. "So is Saffrona."

"*Vaminos tan pronto!*" Saffrona agreed. "Before somebody see us!"

"Let's get outa here, then," Longarm said. "In a minute these prisoners are going to be getting all stirred up."

It took him three tries to find the key that fitted the lock on the cell door, and the babble of voices from the other cells had grown louder as each minute ticked away.

"See if you can get 'em tamed down, Gato," Longarm told his friend. "If they start raising a ruckus, we're going to be in real trouble!"

"*Oigame, amigos!*" El Gato called. "*No hace ruido!*"

"*No quieremos morir, algun mas que tu!*" one of the prisoners shouted. "*Tomenos contigo!*"

"*Es impossible!*" El Gato replied. Then he said in a half-whisper to Longarm, "They want out, too. If we don't open their cells, we'll be in trouble!"

Longarm realized at once that he had no real choice and that a decision must be made quickly. He told El Gato, "Tell 'em we'll give 'em the jailer's keys if they'll promise to keep quiet long enough for us to get outa here!"

150

"Oigame!" El Gato said. *"No puede vaminos contigos, pero date los llaves si callate ahorita!"*

Suddenly the prisoners fell quiet, then one of them asked, *"Como vaminos? Los Rurales—"*

"Chinga los Rurales!" El Gato broke in. *"Tomelos que ofrece o callate!"*

Out of the silence that followed El Gato's threat, one of the prisoners said, *"Bueno! Es agredable!"*

A babble of agreement came from the other cells. El Gato turned back to Longarm.

"They'll take our offer," he said. "But I know damned well they won't wait long enough for us to get clear of this place before they let themselves out."

"It looks to me like that's a chance we just got to take," Longarm replied. "I figured I might be spotted if I brought the horses with me, so we got to go clear back to the stable and then come back to the road. The nags are saddled and ready to ride, but they're back at the stable."

Until now, Saffrona had listened in silence. She broke in to say, "Geev them the keys queeck, Long-arm! We must go fast, or the Rurales weel be wake up!"

One of the prisoners called out, *"Danos pistolas, tambien?"*

"No tenemos!" El Gate replied.

With his limited knowledge of Spanish, Longarm had not been able to follow all of the discussion between the prisoners and El Gato, but this he understood. He raised his voice to be heard above the buzz of conversation that had broken out among the prisoners after the demand for weapons and called, "The jailer's got a rifle and pistol. We'll leave 'em for you if you don't use 'em before we got time to get away!"

Quickly, El Gato translated the offer, and the men in the cells fell quiet. At last one of them answered.

"Bueno. We stay quiet *minuto tan minuto,* you leave the guns!"

Almost before the prisoner had finished speaking, running footsteps sounded on the hard ground outside the door. The yellow glow of a lantern outlined the door's opening, then Novalo ran in, his revolver in his hand.

"Que pase aqui?" the Rurale captain shouted angrily. He saw Longarm and brought up his pistol.

Longarm had started to draw the instant he saw the Rurale commander. His Colt barked before Novalo could level his own weapon. Novalo's body jerked with the impact of the slug and then began crumbling to the ground.

Chapter 15

For an instant following Longarm's shot the jail was deadly silent. Then one of the prisoners shouted, *"Viva el Americano! He muertado Novalo!"*

Suddenly the jail was filled with noise as the men in the cells shouted and cheered wildly.

"Shut up!" Longarm called, but his voice was lost in the tumult of sound.

El Gato added his voice to Longarm's, yelling, *"Callate! Callate, amigos!"*

If the prisoners heard him above their boisterous shouting, they paid no attention. Longarm had been thinking furiously since firing the shot that had triggered their cries of joy. Now he put his mouth close to El Gato's ear and said loudly enough to be heard above the roar, "Let 'em yell a minute. This might—"

"But the Rurales!" El Gato protested. "This shouting will bring them here quickly!"

"Not fast enough to hurt us, if we get moving! Now, make the most of what little time we got, *amigo!* Pick up Novalo's pistol. I imagine it's a pretty good one. Keep it for yourself, let the prisoners have the guard's along with his rifle. But don't give them the keys yet!"

El Gato had faced danger beside Longarm before, and knew that his old friend must have some plan in mind. He hurried to Novalo's body and took the Smith & Wesson .44 that had fallen from the dead man's hand. Then he picked up the rifle beside the unconscious guard and yanked the pistol from his holster. Moving like the cat from which his nickname had been taken, he rejoined Longarm.

"Now what do we do?" he asked.

"You tell them fellows in the cells we'll give 'em the guard's rifle and pistol if they'll fight off the Rurales while we run for the horses. Make it sound like they owe it to us, if you can!"

By now the first flood of exhilaration was beginning to ebb a bit. This time when El Gato shouted *"Callate, amigos!"* the men in the cells subsided, then grew silent.

Even before they were completely quiet, El Gato was exhorting them, and they listened quietly until he'd delivered Longarm's message. When he fell silent a few of the prisoners yelled their loud approval. Then, in the moment of silence that followed their outburst, one of them called out to his fellows.

"Ayudanos!" he shouted. *"Son muertos algun vez! Morimos los Rurales!"*

This time the approving cries were even louder than before. El Gato turned to Longarm and raised his voice loudly enough to be heard above the din.

"They will help!" he said. "Now, let us go quickly!"

Longarm wasted no more time. Though no more than two or three minutes had passed since the night's silence was broken by the shot that brought Novalo down, cries of alarm were sounding from the houses nearest the jail. Even as El Gato spoke, the shouts were beginning to spread through the settlement. Tossing the jailer's keys into the cell across from the one El Gato had occupied, Longarm gave Saffrona and El Gato a shove that started them moving toward the door.

Although the moonless sky provided only a faint starglow, the darkness was not as dense as it had been inside the jail. Longarm took a quick look around as they stopped outside the door. A scattering of lights now showed in the shantytown and against them the figures of the Rurales moving toward the cleared area showed as black silhouettes. The Rurales were running toward the headquarters building, where lighted windows glowed.

"Move fast!" Longarm told his companions. "If we can get to the stable before they figure out what's happening, we still got a good chance to get away!"

"We must keep close together!" El Gato warned.

"Can you keep up, Saffrona?" Longarm asked.

"Do not worry," she replied. "I weel stay weeth you! I do not want to dic!"

Longarm started moving, keeping in the deep shadow along the side of the jail. Over his shoulder, he said, "If any of them men tries to stop us, you do the talking, Gato. With a little bit of help from Lady Luck, we might be able to get away yet!"

More and more lamps were being lighted in the shanties as the three made their way against the stream of Rurales running toward the headquarters. Longarm looked back. A few of the Rurales were now clustered in front of the jail's door. Before Longarm could turn his eyes away, the windows of the jail were lighted with muzzle-blasts from its interior. Then more shots rang out, fired by the Rurales. The shots cut sharply through the shouts of the more distant men who were milling around the headquarters.

"They have found the jail door open!" El Gato called to Longarm. "It will not be long now before they will understand what has happened!"

"We're better'n halfway to the stable now," Longarm said. "Once we get on the horses, we can make it!"

Though time seemed to be standing still as they ran through the darkness, the three finally reached the stable. At the jail, the gunfire had been reduced to single wide-spaced shots by then, and ahead of them the dark forms of only a few stragglers were now visible, moving from the shanties toward the headquarters.

Longarm said to El Gato, "You can see in the dark a lot better 'n I can. Me and Saffrona'll wait outside. You go in and lead the horses out."

El Gato disappeared into the stable. Longarm ran to the stable's wide double doors and began swinging them open. Within a few moments, El Gato came out, leading the horses. Longarm picked up Saffrona and swung her into the saddle of one of them. El Gato already had one foot in the saddle of another, and it took Longarm only an eye-wink to mount the cavalry horse.

"Cut right across through them shanties on a slant towards the road!" Longarm called. "If them Rurales up by the headquarters sees us, they ain't going to shoot so free if we're in amongst them houses they live in!"

Keeping as close together as possible, they moved out in single file, with Longarm in the lead. He saw no chance now of taking the shortest path to the road, and led them toward the shantytown. To take advantage of the protection offered by the hovels, Longarm headed into the group of hovels on a long slant that would take them to the road at a point less than a quarter of a mile beyond the settlement.

Picking a path through the shacks and tents slowed their progress severely. Longarm divided his attention between the job of finding open passage for the horses in the maze of dwellings and trying to keep an eye on the activity around the headquarters building. Lights were showing in all its windows and doors, and the black silhouettes of men moving around told him that the Rurales had at last discovered that Novalo was missing.

More lights were bobbing around the jail now. The prisoners inside were firing less and less often, conserving their small supply of ammunition, and the combat-wise Rurales were wasting as few shells as possible on the men confined in the thick, bullet-proof stone walls of the fortress-like building. The pattern of the shooting told Longarm that the jail's inmates must be down to their last few rounds.

"We got to put on speed," he told his companions. "That bunch up at the headquarters is sure to've found out by now that Novalo ain't around, and them prisoners can't have more'n a shot or two left in their guns. In just another few minutes the Rurales'll have 'em rooted out."

Though all three of them flailed at the horses' flanks with their heels, the animals could only make slow progress as they wound in and out between the shantytown's closely spaced buildings. The shooting at the jail had stopped now. A short time later, when lights started glowing around the jail, a stream of Rurales, some of them carrying lanterns, started toward the headquarters building. As soon as the first of them reached it, faint cries of anger reached the fugitives.

Longarm translated the cries easily, and knew what they told: the Rurales who had been assembling at the headquarters now knew about Novalo's death, and the sergeants had taken command to organize them in pursuit.

"We ain't going to get as much of a lead on them Rurales as I figured we would," he told El Gato. "We'll have to stretch a mite if we're going to beat 'em to the Rio Grande."

"We will be able to go faster when we reach the road," El Gato reminded him. "And they must saddle their horses before they can start after us. We still have enough time."

"Oh, we'll open up some more space between us and them once we get to the road. But they got one edge on us. They're sure to know the country better'n we do."

"All that we need to do is keep going east as fast as we can," El Gato said.

Saffrona had been silent while Longarm and El Gato were talking. Now she broke in to say, "Thees road I know better as you do. A few *kilometros* ahead, there ees place where eet curves and goes on to Ojinago. If we can reach the curve before the Rurales catch up weeth us, we can ride weeth no trouble straight to the reever."

"Figuring they'll keep on following the road," Longarm

157

nodded. "Which I reckon is what they'd do. They'd expect us to make a beeline for the bridge at Ojinaga. We'll try to shake 'em off our tails when we get to that old road, then. It's about the best bet we got."

Longarm turned to look back at the Rurale headquarters. The lights were no longer clustered around it in the numbers he'd seen before. A line of bobbing lanterns showed that a number of the men were starting toward the corrals.

"Let's cut off to the left in a straight line and get outa this mess of tents and stuff as soon as we can," he said. "We'll make better time riding over open country."

Reining toward the clear ground beyond the shanty-town, they soon pushed through the entangling traps of the tents and shanties. Though they no longer had to worry about avoiding the buildings and keeping their mounts from getting entangled in tent guy-ropes, they found that the going was very little better. The earth here was soft and broken, cut by rain-washed gullies and dotted with clumps of cactus and bushy *chaparro* that in the night were visible only as darker blobs against the dark ground.

Time after time the horses stumbled as their hooves plunged into a crack in the soil or a gully cut by rainwater rushing down the long slope, or veered sharply to avoid brush or a boulder. Long before they'd reached the crest of the long ripple of upthrust earth the horses were beginning to breathe hard.

As the distance between them and the Rurale head-quarters increased it also became harder and harder to tell what the Rurales were doing. All that was visible at times were the moving lights that told of confusion and hasty organization. Then they started up a long slope that took them to a high ridge from which they could look down at the activity behind them.

"When we get to the top of this rise, we better stop and let the horses have a breather," Longarm told his companions. "It's as good a place to pull up as any. It'll give us a chance to look back and try to study out what the Rurales is up to."

They reached the crest of the long upslope at last and reined in, then twisted in their saddles to look back at the headquarters. Though the headquarters building still blazed with lamplight from all its windows, there were fewer lights showing around the jail. Though the shanties beyond were almost indistinguishable in the dark and distance, most of them were now lighted.

It was obvious even from a distance that the center of activity had shifted to the stables. There the sides of the building reflected a large fire the Rurales had kindled, and the black forms of moving men were silhouetted against it. On the opposite side a black shadow stretched, spreading across the shantytown and hiding the activity that must be going on among the dwellings there, for here and there patches of light and moving dots of lantern light indicated that the place was a beehive of activity.

"I'm surprised they ain't taken after us yet," Longarm commented to El Gato. "We just better be glad them Mexicans don't move like the Texas Rangers does. If it was Rangers down there, we'd still be running with them right on our tails by now."

"They have had no time to think yet, *amigo*," El Gato pointed out. "It's night, most of them were in bed, and they have only the sergeants to command them, with Novalo dead."

"Reckon you're right," Longarm agreed. Now that he had seen the confusion that still gripped the Rurales, he had no hesitation about taking out a cigar and lighting it. "All the same, it'd seem to me that a few of 'em would've figured out what we done and be coming after us."

"They weel not geeve up when they start," Saffrona warned. "But we must not stop long here. There ees steel many miles to go to Ojinaga and the reever."

"I couldn't've said it better myself, Saffrona," Longarm replied. "And I guess the horses has rested long enough.

159

Come on, we'll move along, but I reckon it's safe enough now for us to cut over towards where we can pick up the road."

El Gato nodded agreement. "As you said a moment ago, they were a very long time in starting. We will be safe doing that, but we must not stay on the road too long. They will be expecting us to head for Ojinaga, I am sure."

"Momento!" Saffrona exclaimed. "I am theenk of sometheeng maybe weel help us!"

"I'm ready to listen to anything that'll get us safe across the Rio Grande," Longarm said. "Go ahead."

"Maybe we do not go to Ojinaga," she said. "Thees ees fool Rurales, no?"

"I'd imagine it would," Longarm told her. "But that's the only place there's a road to where we can cross the river. Or at least it's the only place I seen on all the maps I've looked at."

"Ees not true, Long-arm. There ees small trail made een days when Santa Ana ees make so much robbing from the *ricos,* and they are run to your country. The road to Ojinaga ees new one they make to build breedge where river ees more narrower."

"And it forks off this one?" When Saffrona nodded, he went on, "I guess you'd know where to pick it up?"

"De verdad," she nodded. "When I am child, I go over eet many times."

"And the Rurales don't know about it?"

"Quien sabe?" Saffrona shrugged. "Ees make no matter eef they do. We weel get to reever faster eef we are take eet."

"You're sure you know how to find the cutoff, even in the dark?" Longarm persisted.

"Seguro," she nodded. "I weel see eet, do not to worry."

"Then I'd say we'd better take it," El Gato put in.

"That's my idea, too," Longarm agreed. "The Rurales ain't going to look for us to be heading no place but Ojinaga. If we can give 'em the slip by taking that old road, let's go, while we still got a chance to get to it before daylight."

They reached the road to Ojinaga a quarter of an hour later. Both the danger of exhausting the horses and lack of knowledge of the terrain had kept Longarm from setting too fast a pace before. Once on the road, the horses refreshed after the period of slow, careful travel, they could speed up. Longarm looked back now and then, but he could see no signs as yet that the Rurales were catching up with them.

With a well-defined road to follow, and no further danger that one of the horses would be disabled by a misstep in the dark, Longarm now stepped up their pace. He pushed his cavalry mount to a canter, a faster gait yet one which would not tire the horses so quickly nor be as jarring to the riders as would a full gallop.

They moved steadily, their eyes now accustomed to the darkness, until the horses began to tire. One or another of the animals would begin to slow down, or stumble occasionally, even though there was no obstacle that could have tripped a hoof. When Longarm felt the sides of his mount starting to heave and saw that the animal's head was starting to droop, he reined in again.

"Them Rurales ain't going to be able to move any faster'n we are," he said. "A horse is a horse, and all of 'em gets tired when they been pushed as hard as we been pushing these. Let's give 'em another breather."

As they reined in, he dismounted and the others did the same. They said nothing for a moment while they walked back and forth along the road to ease legs aching from saddle-cramp. From time to time they walked the horses back and forth for a few minutes, to keep their leg muscles from setting up, but the animals were more accustomed than their riders to the strain.

Though all of them were very conscious that the Rurales could not be more than a few miles behind them, none of the three mentioned their pursuers. In fact, they talked very little. Even the usually ebullient El Gato seemed to have lost the desire for idle conversation. When Longarm decided that the mounts had rested enough, he swung into the saddle silently, and Saffrona and El Gato were equally subdued as they got back on their horses and followed him.

Twice more during the next two hours, Longarm halted to rest the horses. The animals were tiring now. Their exhaustion showed in their drooping heads and the way the muscles in their legs trembled during the brief rest periods. The sky ahead was beginning to brighten enough to define the rim of the eastern horizon and Longarm was thinking of calling for another rest stop when Saffrona called to him.

"Go slow, Long-arm! We are close now to the place where ees the old road!"

Longarm reined the cavalry horse to a walk and Saffrona and El Gato pulled up closer until the three were riding almost shoulder to shoulder. They had gone only a few hundred yards when she gave a wordless exclamation of satisfaction, then turned to Longarm and pointed.

"Here ees place old road come een," she said.

Longarm looked ahead, but in the gloom of pre-dawn he could see nothing but the eastern horizon and the brightening sky. He asked Saffrona, "You're sure about it?"

"Ees place," she repeated, pointing to an unusual domed formation, barely visible as a hump against the sky, that rose beyond the road and perhaps a half-mile ahead. "Ees that place I am remember. Es where always we stop and have the *tentempie* when weeth *mi familia* we veeset *abuelitos.*"

Out of deference to Longarm's scanty knowledge of Spanish, El Gato and Saffrona had been speaking English while they were with him, but now El Gato dropped into their common tongue as he asked, *"Es de tuyo, este pais?"*

"Sí," she nodded. *"Nacio en el rancho de mi padre antes el tiempo de Diaz. Pero—"* she shrugged.

162

"Es bastante," El Gato nodded. *"Conozco todo el otro."*

Saffrona turned back to Longarm and said, "I am sure. Ees trail, we weel find eet."

El Gato had already kneed his horse off the road and was walking the animal along its edge, peering at the ground. He had covered perhaps fifty yards in his slow scrutiny when he called, "Saffrona's right, Longarm! There are signs along here of an old road that runs past that hump she pointed to."

"That's all we need, I guess," Longarm replied. "Come on, Saffrona. Let's go."

They joined El Gato and the three of them moved along the ghostly trace of the old road. They kept their horses at a slow walk, which gave them time to watch the terrain ahead and veer away from the gullies that creased its surface and the clumps of cactus and *chaparro* that had found root in the old roadbed. They had covered less than a quarter of a mile when the distant drum of hoofbeats broke the silence of the pre-dawn gloom.

"That's got to be the Rurales!" Longarm exclaimed.

He looked around, trying to locate a hiding place. The only place that offered any shelter at all was the big hump Saffrona had used as a landmark.

Turning to Saffrona and El Gato, he went on, "Let's go! If we can make it around to the other side of that hump before they spot us, chances are they'll ride on past and go all the way to Ojinaga before they find out they've lost us!"

· Chapter 16

Wheeling their horses, they started for the high knoll. The abandoned road had been used by wagons and *carretas* for so many years that it was little more than a pair of deep ruts divided by a ridge as high as a man's knee. After his horse had slipped on the eroded ruts two or three times and nearly fallen, Longarm pulled the animal off the trace and rode on the almost equally eroded soil beside it. Glancing back, he saw that El Gato and Saffrona were following his example.

Behind them, the hoofbeats were growing steadily louder. They reached the base of the big knoll and reined their horses toward its shelter. Glancing back through the grey light, Longarm saw the Rurales. There were perhaps twenty of them, galloping hell for leather. Like all the Rurales Longarm had seen during his cases in Mexico, they were heavily armed. Almost to a man they wore crossed bandoliers filled with rifle ammunition. Each of them carried a revolver in a hip holster and some sported holsters on both hips. To a man they wore the high-crowned gold-embroidered sombreros with upturned brims and the gold-embroidered black vests that had become a Rurale trademark.

Longarm's horse rounded the last few yards of the curve needed to hide him and his companions, and he could no longer see their pursuers.

Thudding hoofbeats sounding loud and then fading told

Longarm what he could not see. In their haste to catch up with their quarry, the Rurales had paid no attention to the old road, nor had they seen any hoofprints that might have been left by the fugitives' horses on the hard soil. As fast as they could ride, they were pushing on to Ojinaga.

"Looks like we're gonna be rid of them fellows," Longarm observed as the hoofbeats died away to silence. "And I don't aim to make out like I'm sorry."

"They weel be back to look for us when they find we do not arrive in Ojinaga," Saffrona warned him.

"Saffrona is right, Longarm," El Gato agreed. "I have learned one thing about the Rurales after the many years I have spent dodging them. They do not give up quickly."

"Ees true," Saffrona seconded. "I know them better as you. *Los Rurales* are like *cuero crudo*."

"Don't worry," El Gato told her. "Longarm and I have a touch of rawhide in us, too. But you know the country better than I do. How far do they have to go to reach Ojinaga?"

"Two, three hour." She frowned. "Ees good road."

"They'll have to get there first, then traipse all the way back here," Longarm reminded his friend. "By that time we oughta be across the Rio Grande. Now, we better start moving. We're still too close to that road for my liking."

Now that they felt it was safe to move at a slower pace, they did not push the horses as they started out. The old wagon road was easy to follow, even though its deep twin ruts had been unused for so many years that the road itself had blended with the landscape.

In places where the infrequent but heavy rains had washed out the ruts and made them into tiny hollows, cacti and *chaparro* had found root, to begin Nature's endless job of restoring to its natural state any changes made by man. Over long straight and level stretches, the twin ruts were barely visible now, but on the small humped ridges that they frequently encountered, the ruts were still deep enough to be used as guides.

They moved steadily ahead while the sun climbed the sky, and they had traveled for perhaps two hours when Saffrona said to Longarm, "Weel we not rest now before we are get to the reever? I am veree, veree tired."

"I guess we might as well pull up again," he nodded. "Even if we didn't need to rest ourselves, the horses sure do. Come right down to it, we better take off their bridles and let 'em graze, if they can find anything to chew on. That sun's getting right hot, and it can't do much but get hotter."

Dismounting, they loosened the bridle straps and took the bits out of the mouths of the horses. The animals stood quietly for a moment, then began moving slowly around, nuzzling the scanty growth in search of something edible.

"I don't reckon there's a creek or a spring anywhere up ahead of us, is there?" Longarm asked Saffrona. "Them nags is going to be hurting for water before too long."

She shook her head. "Ees no water before the reever. Een old days when I travel weeth *familia, mi papacito* ees bring leetle barrel water een cart."

"I guess that means the nags is just going to have to go dry till we get to the river, then," Longarm said. "Too bad, but it can't be helped. We'll just have to go easy on running 'em, that's all."

"How much farther is it?" El Gato asked Saffrona.

"Ees long way. Ees not easy to travel over such country as ahead of us now. Eef we go fast, maybe we weel get there before night."

"If we don't let these horses rest while we got a chance, we might not get there at all, unless we like walking," Longarm warned. "And walking ain't one of the things I do best."

They began walking around aimlessly, trying to get the kinks out of their legs. Saffrona was the first to lie down. She found a small stretch of sandy soil unbroken by rocks or humps of hard earth and dropped to the ground, pillowing her head on a folded arm.

Saffrona looked so comfortable that Longarm and El Gato soon followed her example, though they sat with folded legs rather than lying on the ground. Too tired to talk, they sat silently, watching the sun creep higher, looking at the huge expanse of nearly barren earth that stretched in all directions as far as they could see.

In the silence of the warm morning, the whickering of one of the horses sounded as loud as a shout. Longarm and El Gato looked at the animal. It was one of the horses Longarm had gotten from the Rurales' corral. Now it was standing with its neck arched and its head held high as though smelling the warm breeze.

"There's got to be something plaguing that animal," Longarm frowned. "Either it's hearing something or smelling something that we can't."

"*Verdad,*" El Gato agreed. "And the only thing that occurs to me is that it smells another horse close by."

The two got to their feet. Saffrona had dropped off to sleep. She was lying stretched out a short distance away, one arm thrown over her eyes to blot out the sun.

Longarm glanced at the sky. "Them Rurales ain't had time to get to Ojinaga and back." He frowned thoughtfully. "But since we got on this misbegotten road, we ain't seen any sign that it's been used since Hector was a pup."

"That does not mean it has been forgotten," El Gato pointed out. "There may be some of the Rurales who remember it."

"That ain't likely," Longarm objected. "They was right close to us when we pulled off onto it. They'd've caught up with us before now if they'd turned off, close as they were behind us when we switched onto it."

"Then consider another possibility," El Gato went on. "Suppose that on the road the Rurales met a traveler coming from Ojinaga, and he told them that he had not seen us. They would know then that we had turned off."

"I guess it could've been that way," Longarm agreed.

"Saffrona is not likely to be the only one who knows of

this road," El Gato continued. "Perhaps one of the Rurales knew of it, too, and suddenly realized that we could have taken it."

Again Longarm nodded. "I guess it could've been one as easy as the other. But more'n likely they just figured they could cover more ground faster if they split up and scattered. And we sure didn't take time trying to hide our trail. Hard as this ground is, we've left tracks."

"Think of the time we would have wasted trying to hide them!"

"Well, it ain't all that important how they got on our tails. The fact is, we got to start running again."

"Unless we choose to fight," El Gato reminded him. "Not that we should; this flat country is not good for us to fight in. Besides, we have only one rifle between us. To fight here would be foolish."

"I wouldn't argue that a minute, Gato. A man can see to hell and gone any direction he wants to look. But it sure cuts against my grain for us to start running again."

"I agree," El Gato nodded. "But before we decide what the best thing is to do, should we not find out what we are facing?"

"I'll slip back and take a look. You wake up Saffrona and push on. I'll catch up with you."

Longarm wasted no time. He replaced his horse's bridle and swung into the saddle. Angling away from the trace they had been following, he started back toward the main road.

Not sure what he would be facing, Longarm took his time. When he had gotten a quarter of a mile from the trace he turned and rode parallel to the ghost-road, keeping the cavalry mount at a slow walk that gave him plenty of time to scan his surroundings in all directions. He had covered perhaps two miles when his horse raised its head and pricked up its ears, as a horse will do when its keen sense of smell and hearing detects a strange animal in its vicinity.

Longarm was well aware of the limitations of human

vision. A man on foot in flat open country could see only three to four miles, while a man in the saddle could see almost twice as far. By standing in his stirrups he could add at least an additional half-mile or so to his field of view, and yet to another rider as short a distance as three to four miles away his head would appear to be nothing more than a feature of the landscape, a small bump rising on the horizon's ragged rim.

Standing up in his stirrups, he examined the barren vista ahead, swiveling his head with slow deliberation to reduce the chances that he would be noticed. At the extreme range of his vision he saw six riders moving toward him. The distance was too great and even the scant vegetation too dense for him to make out any details of their clothing or their features, but because they were spread out in a rough line with the abandoned trace cutting its center, he was certain that he was looking at a detachment of Rurales.

There was no point in wasting time. Longarm eased back into the saddle and hunched over the horse's neck. Leaving the reins slack, he guided the animal with his booted toes into a slow curve that turned him back on the trace. Keeping to his crouched position, he nudged the horse ahead. Only after he had covered almost a mile and he could see his companions ahead did he sit erect again and urge the horse to a gallop.

El Gato and Saffrona were letting their horses walk. They wheeled around when they heard the cavalry mount's hoofbeats drumming on the hard-baked ground and waited for him to come up to them.

"It was Rurales, all right," he said as he reined in. "Six of 'em, heading towards us."

"Fast?" El Gato asked.

"No. They've found our tracks back a ways, and they're following 'em, but they ain't seen us yet."

"They are far behind us, then?" Saffrona asked.

"Far enough so they ain't going to spot us right away."

"We must go faster," El Gato said.

"I already figured that out," Longarm replied. Turning to Saffrona, he asked, "I don't guess there's anyplace between here and the Rio Grande where we can hole up? A canyon, a mesa, anything like that?"

She shook her head. "Ees no place to hide. We can only run." Then she frowned, was silent for a moment, and added, "I do not know eef the house of my family ees steel stand. But ees only small adobe."

"You got any idea how far it is?" he asked.

"Ees maybe seex, eight miles. Right by reever."

"That'd be the Rio Grande?" When Saffrona nodded, Longarm went on, "A shelter ain't going to help us much, if it's that close to the river. Once we get there, we won't need a place to hole up. We'll just go on across it."

"They might follow us," El Gato objected. "The Rurales do such things, you know. They do not worry about such a small matter as a boundary line."

"Oh, sure," Longarm agreed. "But even with what guns we got, once we're on the other side of the Rio Grande, we oughta be able to keep 'em from crossing."

"If we're going to go, we'd better move, then," El Gato suggested.

Longarm toed his horse and as the big chestnut started moving he turned to say to his companions, "If we put on a little steam, we oughta beat 'em there. The horses are pretty fresh, and the nags them Rurales is riding has been on the run since they taken after us. Let's go."

Keeping to the side of the rutted trace, they urged their horses ahead. They had been riding for half an hour when they reached a point where the land began to tilt upward. For a mile or more ahead they could see the ground rising gently in long, rippling waves. The earth was completely barren ahead. Not even cacti grew on the rippled stretch that now lay in front of them. The only mark on the ripples was the narrow streak that marked the remnants of the trail. There was no vegetation at all on the long slope, and as they started up the rise ahead the horses began to move more slowly.

Looking back, Longarm could see no sign of the Rurales yet, and he devoted all his attention to the terrain. It was made tricky by the changed contours of the ground, for as they rode up the slope the ripples grew wider and their edges deeper. The spacing of the patterned contours that stretched across the surface at right angles to their course were now longer and their uppermost side was higher.

This change in spacing did not match the gait the horses had been maintaining so effortlessly and steadily. With the crests of the wrinkled surface farther apart and rising higher, the horses could no longer maintain a steady ground-covering lope, but were forced to break stride between the rises. Then, as they neared the crest of the long upslope, a rifle cracked behind them and a slug kicked up dust and small clods of dirt between the animals ridden by Longarm and Saffrona.

Longarm's cavalry-trained mount did not falter or break stride, but the pony from the Rurales' corral shied and started bucking. Its action caught Saffrona by surprise, and she almost fell. Longarm reined over sharply and grabbed her flailing arm to hold her in the saddle. The horse did not buck again, and Saffrona was able to bring it under control again just before another shot sounded and a bullet cut the air above their heads.

Longarm had glanced back to see where the first shot came from. He saw that two of the six Rurales had reached the bottom of the long slope. Both of them had pulled the rifles from their saddle scabbards. As Longarm watched, one of the guns cracked and its bullet tore into the hard soil inches from the hind hooves of the cavalry horse.

Longarm pulled his rifle out of its saddle scabbard. He did not shoulder the weapon, but fought down the temptation to reply, for he knew his Winchester had the range that

171

the carbines of the Rurales lacked. Instead, he called to El Gato, "Come over here and give Saffrona a hand! She's got a skittish horse!"

As El Gato responded with a twitch of his reins, the second Rurale fired, and hot lead whistled past Longarm's head.

"Let's get over that hump as fast as we can!" Longarm urged when he saw El Gato's hand close over Saffrona's reins. "That old farmhouse Saffrona told us about oughta be on the other side of this slope, but even if it ain't close enough for us to get to it, maybe the drop-off's steep enough to get us outa their line of fire!"

As he saw that El Gato and Saffrona were within a stride of the crest, he turned back to glance at the Rurales, and found that the four remaining members of the party had joined the first two. Longarm shouldered the Winchester and shot quickly. The Rurale who was in his sights jerked in his saddle, but did not fall. Longarm was at the crest of the rise now. He braced himself as the cavalry mount plunged down the steep grade that led to a stream of green-gray water flowing at its base.

Ahead of him, Longarm saw that El Gato and Saffrona had already started down the steep slope. He gave the horse its head and the animal plunged down the hard slanting soil, overtaking El Gato and Saffrona, whose horses by now were close to the bottom of the twenty-foot-high rise.

"This has got to be the Rio Grande!" Longarm called as his horse slid past them, its hindquarters low, its forelegs braced stiffly. "We'll be all right soon as we get across it!"

Longarm's horse hit the water and tried to dig in its rear hooves to keep from sliding into the stream, but the momentum it had gained during the downward slide carried it into the water. When he saw that the horse was going into the water, Longarm kicked out of his stirrups, ready to jump if the animal fell, but the soft silt of the riverbed checked its plunge gently. For a moment the horse floundered, then it regained its balance and stood quietly.

A few feet away, the mounts carrying El Gato and Saffrona were standing quietly. Longarm pointed to the gentle slope of the opposite bank and dug his heels into the chestnut's flank. With a great deal of splashing in the foot-deep water, the horse crossed the stream and made its way up the bank. Beside him, the other horses were emerging from the water.

"It feels right good to be back in the U. S.," Longarm said as they pulled up beside him. "Now them Rurales won't lay a hand on us. They know what'll happen to 'em if they do."

"I do not ondestan' thees thing," Saffrona said. "But we are steel een Mexico, Long-arm. Look. There is the house of my *familia,* and eet ees where eet has always stand."

For the first time, Longarm noticed the spreading locust tree that stood a dozen yards from the bank, its foliage half-shielding the roofless, crumbling adobe walls of what had once been a house.

"You are sure that's the house your family lived in?" El Gato asked her.

"*Seguro que sí,*" she said firmly. "Thees ees not a theeng I am to forget. And eet was never in United States, ees in Mexico always."

"Whatever country it's in, we better make for it fast!" Longarm told them. "Because in just about two more minutes them Rurales is going to get to the top of that rise, and once they see us, they won't give two hoots in hell whether we're in the U. S. or Mexico. They're going to start shooting!"

Spurring up the gentle slope that led to the ruined house, they rode around its broken, tumbling walls to a spot where the horses would be hidden. They had barely gotten to shelter when they heard the Rurales galloping up. The sound of their horses' hoofbeats stopped abruptly.

"Sounds like they stopped on the other side of the river," Longarm said. "Gato, you better just sorta disappear. Find a hidey-hole fast. Me and Saffrona won't be in as bad trouble as you would, if they take us back."

"I wouldn't desert you, old friend!" El Gato protested. "I've beaten the Rurales too many times to fear them!"

"Don't argue with me!" Longarm told him. He was pulling his Winchester from its saddle scabbard as he spoke. "Find a hidey-hole and pull the top in after you! Me and Saffrona'll be all right! Now, git! Saffrona, you come on with me!"

Not stopping to watch El Gato, Longarm led Saffrona into the tumbledown roofless house. A corner section of the broken wall gave them cover as they moved carefully to the side nearest the stream. Beyond its banks they could hear the voices of the Rurales calling to one another.

"We better show ourselves," Longarm said. "It ain't likely they'll shoot right now. They want El Gato worse than they do us. We'll stall and give him time to get hid."

By this time, Longarm and Saffrona had gained the shelter provided by the corner of the wall. Peering carefully around one of its slanting, broken ends, Longarm saw the six Rurales sitting on their horses at the edge of the steep bank on the opposite side of the stream. Longarm could read the puzzlement in their faces, but he knew that within a very few moments it would become apparent to the Rurales where he and Saffrona were hiding. He decided to take the bull by the horns.

"You stay hid unless I need you to tell me what they're saying," he told her.

"I weel do *traduccion*," Saffrona nodded. "Maybe so they know me, they leesten easier."

Raising his voice, Longarm called, "You men listen! I'm a United States deputy marshal, and I got a couple of prisoners over here! You and me had better talk instead of shooting, or we'll both be in trouble!"

From the opposite bank one of the Rurales replied, "You are the one called Long, no?"

174

"That's right," Longarm answered. "And I ain't looking for trouble, but there's going to be some if we don't settle this peaceful."

For a moment the Rurales were silent. Then the man who'd spoken before called, "We have notheeng to talk about! You have prisoner who ees belong to us! Geeve heem up, and we talk then. Eef you do not, we weel come and take heem!"

Chapter 17

"You can see for yourself, there ain't nobody here but me and Saffrona," Longarm called back. "And you know she ain't going to hurt you none!"

"You have *El Anguila del Desierto* weeth you!" the Rurale replied angrily. "He ees get away from *el carcel*, and keel our *comandante!* And we know he ees weeth you because we see heem!"

"He give us the slip, too!" Longarm said. "Hold your fire, now, and we'll step out where you can see us!"

Nodding to Saffrona to follow him, Longarm stepped from the cover of the slanted wall. Saffrona hesitated only a moment before joining him. The Rurales had not dismounted. They were lined up along the high bank on the opposite side of the stream.

"Like I told you, there ain't anybody here but me and her," Longarm went on. "You know how slippery that Eel fellow is. Soon as we got across the river he just sorta disappeared. But even if he was with us, you couldn't touch him now."

"Why you are say that?" the Rurale frowned.

Longarm pointed to the sun-glistening water flowing in the shallow channel between them. "Once you men cross the Rio Grande river, you're in the United States, and on this side you ain't got authority to arrest anybody."

Patting the holstered revolver on his hip, the Rurale

said, "Thees ees what authority we use, eef you do not geeve heem up!"

"Wait a minute, now!" Longarm protested. "You start shooting across the border at somebody on the United States side, and your big *jefe* in Mexico City's going to hear about it! All of you'll be in a mess of trouble, then."

"You are the one who weel be in trouble," the Rurale retorted. "Thees leetle puddle water between us ees not Rio Grande. The reever ees on other side of house."

"You oughta know I wouldn't be fool enough to fall for a yarn like that," Longarm told the Rurale. "Like I said, I ain't looking for a fight, but the minute you move to come after us, the shooting's going to start!"

"Leesten to what I am say, Long!" the Rurale snapped. "Ees not river between us! *El Rio Grande* ees run on other side from house. What ees between us ees leettle fork that shoot from reever five, seex years ago, when ees beg flood."

Before Longarm could reply, Saffrona spoke in a whisper too soft for the Rurales to hear. "I theenk he ees right," she said. "Like I am tell you when we are first get to house, I am never to see reever thees side from eet. Never."

Without taking his eyes off the Rurales, Longarm asked in a half-whisper, "Are you sure about that, Saffrona?"

"Absolutamente!" she said emphatically. "Was *arroyo* here where reever ees now, but eet hold water only after beeg rain."

"Then I better think of something to say real fast," Longarm muttered, "or we'll really be in bad trouble. Not that we ain't now, but I—" He broke off as the Rurale spoke again.

"Who you are talk weeth, *gringo?*" the Rurale demanded. "Ees *El Anguila del Desierto,* no?"

Under his breath, Longarm told Saffrona, "Maybe they'll believe you. Try it, anyhow."

177

Saffrona raised her voice and called, *"Tu mi conocen! No soy El Anguila, verdad?"*

"Conocemos," the man nodded. *"Pero ya conocemos tambien El Anguila!"* Facing Longarm again, the Rurale went on, "What you are say, *gringo?* Geeve us *El Anguila* or we come take heem!"

Longarm could see that he was running out of time, but decided to stall as long as possible. He called back, "I ain't going to say you're lying about this stream in between us not being the Rio Grande, but I'm going to go out in back of the house and look for myself. If I see there's really a river back there, we'll talk about making some kind of deal."

"I weel geev you *tres minutos,"* the Rurale said. "But you weel find reever, thees I tell you true!"

Longarm slid his Colt from its holster and held it out to Saffrona. "You know how to use one of these?" he asked.

"Seguro," she replied. She lifted a corner of her skirt and reached under it to produce an ivory-handled .22 Baby Smith & Wesson. "But you see, I do not need your beeg gun. I am have my own."

"If you was to shoot one of them Rurales with that, he'd likely get up and spank you good," Longarm told her. "Here, take this one." Suddenly it occurred to him that she would do better with her own little shooter than she would with his heavy Colt. Holstering his own weapon, he said, "Suit yourself. Anything you do to keep them stalled will help. But don't be afraid to shoot if they start over here before I get back."

"I am afraid from nobody!" Saffrona said. "These Rurales, they do not scare me. I am see them weeth their pants down."

"You are waste time, *gringo!"* the Rurale warned, his voice sharp and impatient.

"I'll just be a minute," Longarm nodded.

Walking quickly through the fragments of walls that still stood, Longarm went through the skeleton of the house. A wide stretch of baked soil led to a drop-off. As he approached the edge, he could see the sun glinting off water, and it was very obvious that the water was indeed flowing in the Rio Grande's main channel.

Well, old son, this place is just what that damned Rurale said it was. You're on an island, and it belongs to Mexico. So you really got yourself boxed in this time, Longarm told himself silently as he gazed at the roiling water.

He looked along the spit between the true and false channels of the river. It was perhaps a mile long, the decayed house not quite in its center. High weeds and grasses covered the long oval-shaped islet, their dark green foliage a sharp contrast to the grayish green of the river. There were no trees on the spit, no other structures than the house shell.

There sure ain't no way of getting outa this trap, old son, Longarm mused. *About all you can do is go back and stall, give El Gato time to put some distance between him and them Rurales, then throw in the towel.*

A pistol shot sounded, high-pitched, the kind of report that could have come only from Saffrona's little weapon. It was followed by the heavier report of a barking rifle. Then the still air was broken by a volley of rifle shots. Longarm had turned and started running for the house at the first shot. Now he ran even faster.

He drew his Colt as he reached the ruined house and through the openings that had once been closed by doors saw Saffrona lying sprawled on the floor near the corner of the broken outer wall. Her pistol lay beside one outstretched hand. At that instant a rifle barked, but at the sight of Saffrona lying prone Longarm had dived to the buckled floor and started crawling toward her. His rifle was leaning against the wall, and he reached for it.

On the other side of the shallow channel of the false river, he could see the Rurales leaning back in their saddles, holding their rifles in one hand, their reins in the other, as their horses slid down the steep incline toward the water. Longarm got the nearest one in his sights and triggered off a shot. The Rurale fell from his saddle and rolled limply down the steep bank into the water.

All five of the remaining riders were in the stream now, splashing across it. Longarm levered a fresh round into the rifle's chamber and picked the closest Rurale as his target. He got off his second shot, and again the slug went home. Now two of the Rurales were lying in the shallow water, their horses standing over them.

Seeing a third of his force put out of action, the leader turned his horse in the middle of the shallow channel and started back, but the steep bank defeated all the efforts of his horse to mount it.

Longarm glanced at the other three Rurales as he worked the Winchester's lever to slide a fresh shell into the chamber, and saw that they were also trying to get their rearing mounts up the bank, but were having no more success than their commander.

Setting his jaw, Longarm swung the Winchester's muzzle toward the commander, but before he could trigger off the shot the leader shouted to his men.

"Cedeten," he commanded. *"O el gringo matenos enteramente!"*

To underline the leader's command, Longarm fired again, but this time he aimed wide, sending the bullet between two of the men who were still struggling with their horses, trying to get them up the sloping bank across the shallow stream. They let their rifles drop from their shoulders, as did the Rurale who was between them and the commander.

"That's better," Longarm said. "But I'll be nervous till you get rid of them rifles. Toss 'em on the ground, quick!"

When the Rurales did not obey, Longarm looked back at their leader. He said, "You heard me tell them what to do. Maybe they don't understand plain English, so you better remind 'em of what I just said."

His voice trembling with suppressed anger, the leader

said, *"Ponesen los fuisiles al tierra!"*

Reluctantly, the Rurales let their rifles fall. Longarm still was not satisfied.

"Now tell 'em to toss their pistols down, too," he said.

This time the commander's order came too late. His men were already unbuckling their gunbelts and letting them drop at their feet.

"That's better," Longarm said. He stepped from behind the wall now, his Winchester held casually, but in a position where he could shoulder it in an instant, swinging the muzzle in a narrow arc to threaten the four survivors. He said, "Now you can tell 'em to pick up them two dead men. Soon as they get 'em up the bank, the whole bunch of you can cart 'em back to where you come from. Just don't—" He stopped short as the thudding of hoofbeats sounded on the low rise above the false channel, then went on, "I guess that's some more of your outfit coming up. Don't get no ideas about—"

He broke off as he saw the familiar figure of El Gato seated on the horse that appeared on the edge of the bluff. He pulled up and surveyed the Rurales in the cut below him.

"I heard the shots and got here as fast as I could," El Gato said apologetically. He looked at the subdued Rurales, who were picking up the bodies of their fellows, and at the scattered weapons, and added, "I thought you might need help, but it looks like you did a pretty good job of helping yourself."

"It wasn't all that hard," Longarm replied. He took out a cigar and lighted it before adding, "Which ain't to say I couldn't've used some help."

"I hadn't gone very far when I heard the shooting," El Gato explained. "And I thought I'd better come back and see if I could get you to change your mind."

A sigh from the ground beside him drew Longarm's attention before he could say anything to El Gato. He looked down and saw that Saffrona was sitting up. She

181

held one hand pressed to her forehead.

"I figured you was a goner, Saffrona," Longarm said. "But you sure look all right now. You mind telling me what happened?"

"When I see the Rurales are start to cross reever, I am shoot, like you tell me to," she answered. "One of them ees shoot back, but he mees me. The bullet heet wall by my head. Piece of adobe are fall on me, and I am go asleep queeck."

Across the draw, El Gato was sliding his mount down the bank to the water. He reined in at the edge of the draw and began gathering up the Rurales' weapons. Without bothering to unload the guns, he simply tossed them into the water.

Longarm returned his attention to the Rurales. The men had carried the bodies up the steep bank now and were standing by their horses.

"Go on, load them bodies on whatever nag they belong to, and get on back where you come from," Longarm told them. "And if you got any ideas about bringing your friends back here, you might as well change your minds, because by the time you'd get here, we'll be on the American side of the river."

The Rurales busied themselves with the job of lashing the dead men on the backs of their horses. Then, at the command of their leader, they rode off in the direction from which they had come. El Gato had ridden up to the house by now. He dismounted and looked at Longarm.

"I suppose your job here is done?" he asked.

"Well, the only reason I was sent down here was to make sure the Rurales had the real Desert Eel in their lockup," Longarm replied. "And you know how that turned out."

El Gato nodded. "I hope I didn't upset your plans by not being the real one."

"You didn't upset my plans," Longarm said. "But Captain Morales is sure gonna be sorry you wasn't."

"Why is that?"

"Oh, it seems like the Eel robbed a bank down in Toluca, and taken a bunch of papers the captain was saving to give the president. Now that the Eel's dead, I guess the papers is long gone."

"I do not think so," El Gato frowned. "When *El Anguila* and I had our little meeting—his last, of course—he was carrying a great deal of loot. I had small time to look at it, but there were canvas bags with the name of the Toluca bank on them."

"I don't guess you been carrying them around all this time?"

"No. But they are in a safe place. If it will ease your mind, I will see that the papers are delivered to Morales."

"Well, I'd take that real kindly, Gato," Longarm nodded. "It'd really help close my case here." He dug his wallet out and slid the scrap of paper containing Morales's address from behind his badge. "Here's where you can send it. Or take it yourself, if you've got a mind to."

"Consider it done, then." El Gato stood up and extended his hand. "I thank you for my life, my friend."

"Don't make over it a lot," Longarm said, taking the extended hand. "You've done me a good turn or two."

"We will see each other when we meet again, then," El Gato said. *"Vaya con Dios, amigo."*

"Same to you, Gato," Longarm nodded. "Have a good trip, wherever you're going."

Longarm watched while El Gato mounted and rode off, then belatedly remembered Saffrona. He looked around the ruins of the house, but she was nowhere in sight.

"Saffrona!" he called.

When she answered, her voice was distant. It came from the area behind the structure. Longarm walked through the ruins and saw her sitting on the high riverbank, looking out over the greenish water of the Rio Grande. He went to sit down beside her.

"I sorta forgot about you when the shooting started," he

said. "You feeling all right by now?"

"*Tal bueno*. Eet was not hard my head was heet." She turned toward Longarm and he saw a red, swollen bump on one side of her forehead.

"What do you figure to do now, Saffrona?" Longarm asked after they had sat silently for a few moments. "I don't reckon you can go back to the Rurale camp after all the fuss I stirred up."

Saffrona shook her head. "They weel not forget what I have do. Eef I go back, they keel me."

"I'm sorry I got you into a mess the way I did, Saffrona," Longarm said. "I don't guess it was right for me to ask you to help me the way I did."

"Ees not your fault. Ees way theengs happen. But I am already get tired of there when you come," she said. "I am theenk a long time ees time I leeve."

"But you didn't have noplace else in your mind?"

"No. But I do now. I see thees place here, where I am baby, where I am leev till *revolucion*. I theenk I stay here."

"It'd take a lot of work to fix up this house and put in some kind of crop that'd bring you a living," he said.

"I can pay. I have save money."

"I owe you some money myself," Longarm said. "I never did give you the rest of what I promised you. But I will, before I start back."

"You are go back, no?"

"Why, sure. I finished my job here. Now I'll have to head back to Denver."

"Thees ees what I know you are to tell me," Saffrona sighed. "But ees more I want from you than money, Longarm."

"What'd that be?"

"You have not forget," she told him. She turned to face him. The sadness he had seen on her face before had vanished, and now she looked at him with a mischievous smile. "The first time I am see you, I tell you what I am want." Her hand slid caressingly over Longarm's crotch.

"Ees the same I want now."

"Well, now," Longarm said, "I don't have to start back to Denver right this minute, Saffrona. Fact is, it's so late that I wouldn't get far enough today to make no never-mind. And I'm always ready to give a pretty lady anything she wants."

Watch for

LONGARM AND THE TRAIL DRIVE SHAM

ninety-eighth novel in the bold
LONGARM series from Jove

and

LONGARM AND THE LONE STAR MISSION

the next giant LONGARM adventure
featuring the LONE STAR duo

coming in February!